Key to the
Prison

Books by Louise A. Vernon

Title	Subject
The Beggars' Bible	John Wycliffe
The Bible Smuggler	William Tyndale
Doctor in Rags	Paracelsus and Hutterites
A Heart Strangely Warmed	John Wesley
Ink on His Fingers	Johann Gutenberg
Key to the Prison	George Fox and Quakers
The King's Book	King James Version, Bible
The Man Who Laid the Egg	Erasmus
Night Preacher	Menno Simons
Peter and the Pilgrims	English Separatists, Pilgrims
The Secret Church	Anabaptists
Thunderstorm in Church	Martin Luther

Key to the
Prison

Louise A. Vernon
Illustrated by Allan Eitzen

Herald
Press

Scottdale, Pennsylvania
Waterloo, Ontario

KEY TO THE PRISON
Copyright © 1968 by Herald Press, Scottdale, Pa. 15683
    Published simultaneously in Canada by Herald Press,
    Waterloo, Ont. N2L 6H7. All rights reserved
Library of Congress Catalog Card Number: 68-11054
International Standard Book Number: 0-8361-1813-8
Printed in the United States of America

06 05 04 03 02   10 9 8 7 6

To order or request information, please call
1-800-759-4447 (individuals); 1-800-245-7894 (trade).
Website: www.mph.org

Contents

1

Street Preacher

Puzzled and uneasy, Tommy Stafford measured out cow feed in the shed behind the parsonage. In all his twelve years he could not remember such a quiet morning. Why weren't Mother and Father talking? They usually chattered like magpies before Father went to the tiny study and worked on his next sermon. Fourteen-year-old Celia was not up yet, or she would have questioned the silence in her impulsive way.

His chores done, Tommy hurried toward the kitchen, then paused, dreading to go in. To his relief, Father was speaking.

"Elizabeth," he heard Father say, "is it God's will?"

The tense voice did not sound like Father at all. Tommy hesitated, not wanting to eavesdrop, yet not daring to interrupt.

"If I leave," Father went on, "how will you and the children make out? Am I acting selfishly? Is this a temptation or is it divine guidance?"

"Now, Thomas," Mother said in her quiet way, "you must follow your inner voice. It will not mislead you. God will show you the path He wants you to take."

Tommy heard the scrape of a chair. Mother appeared at the back door. "Tommy," she called, "it's market day. Would you and Celia like to go into town?"

Tommy ran into the kitchen. "Oh, Mother, yes!"

"Call Celia then. You'd better start early."

"But, Mother—" Tommy began. It was the day he was to deliver eggs to Widow Buxby at the Golden Lamb Inn, a few miles away.

"I'll take the eggs myself," Mother said, as if reading his mind. "Hurry! Call Celia."

Her urgent tone spurred Tommy upstairs to Celia's room.

"Wake up, Celia. It's market day. Mother said we could go into town." He rumpled his sister's tousled, honey-colored hair.

Wide awake in an instant, Celia wasted no time asking questions. She too must have sensed a special urgency in Mother's offer.

When Tommy and Celia were ready to leave, Mother stopped them at the door. "I want you to do something for me," she said in a low voice. "There's a preacher named George Fox staying at Swarthmoor Hall. If by chance you should see him in town, let me know."

With a puzzled look, Celia nodded. Before she could start asking questions, Tommy pulled her out to the road. Somehow, he felt he and Celia should keep quiet.

"Why would Mother say a thing like that?" Celia asked on the way to town.

Tommy described the puzzling silence that morning. "Maybe she wants him to talk to Father. Have you noticed lately when Father is preaching? He doesn't stand still behind the pulpit. He rocks, like this." Tommy stopped to illustrate. "I think he's trying to decide something."

"Oh, Tommy, for a twelve-year-old you have the oddest ideas sometimes. What's there to decide? Father can preach here in Ulverston for life—that is, if Squire Grantham doesn't get mad at him. Come on. I hear hammering. Someone is putting up a new market stall."

Ahead of them, country folk bustled through the narrow, crooked streets laden with baskets of fruit and vegetables. Tommy and Celia stopped to watch a laborer pull a two-wheeled cart loaded with boards over the cobblestones. He made a sharp turn, and the lumber slid to one side.

A pleasant-faced farmer carrying two heavy baskets paused and looked around. " 'Twould be better if thou didst not speed so fast," he said in a mild tone.

"Mind your own business," the laborer snapped. "You have no right to *thou* me."

One of the cart wheels sank into a rut. The cart tilted and the boards spilled out. The country folk roared with laughter, jeering at the red-faced laborer. No one offered to help right the cart—no one except the farmer. Without a word of reproach, he pulled and tugged at the loose boards, straining to lift them into the cart.

A murmur rose from the onlookers. "He's a Friend."

"A what?" Tommy heard someone ask.

"A Friend—you know. Quakers, they're called, because they tremble under God's power, so I hear."

"Oh, the ones that *thee* and *thou* everybody and take off their hats?"

"That's them. Wonder where they got such queer notions."

When the cart was loaded, the embarrassed but grateful laborer doffed his hat in thanks.

"Hold, friend." The farmer raised his hand in protest. "Take off thy cap to no man—but only to God."

The laborer stared, his hand still on his cap; then he pulled his cart away without a word.

A man near Tommy and Celia grunted. "He's a Quaker, sure enough," he said in a low voice. The others made way for the farmer and his two baskets.

The onlookers murmured among themselves. "I understand Judge Fell's wife, right here in Ulverston, is thicker than thieves with them Quakers—or Friends, as they call themselves," someone stated. "Can't understand why. She's a mighty worthy woman."

Another exclaimed, "That's right. She's done more to help the paupers—and the country's crawling with them—than the justices, the sheriff, and the constables put together. How she ever got mixed up with the Quakers, I couldn't say. I hear she even has their leader, name of George Fox, staying up there at Swarthmoor Hall. I'll wager her troop of lively little ones will make a real Quaker out of him if he stays there very long."

There was an outburst of laughter on all sides. Celia tugged at Tommy's sleeve. "George Fox! That's the one Mother wants to know about. Come on. Look

10

at that crowd up ahead. Someone's giving a speech."

They could not get close enough to see the speaker because of the crowd of people.

"Which one is he?" Tommy asked.

Celia stretched on tiptoe. "I can't see him. There are too many people up front waving their big hats."

An onlooker cried out in a loud voice, "Why did you come here to spoil our market day?"

A deep, resonant voice answered, "Because in markets I see deceitful merchandise and cheating."

"If you're going to preach, preach in a church," someone shouted.

"A steeple house is not a church," the deep voice responded. "The bell calls people together in a steeple house just like a market bell to gather people for the preacher to set forth his wares."

Tommy gasped. "It's a good thing Father isn't hearing this," he told Celia.

"I deny the so-called church," the speaker added.

At these words there were shouts and cries from a hundred throats. Someone flung a stone. Others brandished walking sticks. With a roar, the crowd with one impulse surged forward like a tidal wave and washed over the man who had been speaking.

Celia clung to Tommy, almost crying. "Oh, how terrible! What are they going to do to him? I don't want to see any more. Let's go home." She turned and started to run. Tommy caught up with her. "Celia, do you think that was George Fox?"

Celia shuddered. "It must be, but let's don't tell Mother about what we saw. Wouldn't it be awful to be a street preacher like that? I'm glad Father has a church."

11

At home, the troubled faces of Mother and Father silenced both Tommy and Celia. Supper was a quiet meal. Tommy felt hot, even though there was an edge of coolness to the summer warmth. Uncomfortable with his jacket on, somehow he did not dare make an extra movement. It was as if any unusual motion would start an eruption of some kind, something that Tommy would not be able to stop, nor Celia either, even though she had a sharp tongue and used it. Mother, watchful and quiet, waited for Father to speak. What had happened during the day? What was the decision Father was trying to make?

After supper, Mother and Celia cleared the table. Father did not go to his study. Instead, he sat staring ahead.

Mother broke the silence in a voice hardly more than a whisper. "Have you made a decision, Thomas?"

Father looked up. His brown eyes deepened in color, as if he held back intense feeling. His strong-featured face was set. "Yes, I have. I've talked to the squire."

Tommy held his breath. Everyone knew what a terrible temper the squire had, especially when he was having a gout attack. Squire Grantham's words were as strong as the law around Ulverston.

"I'm leaving the church," Father said.

Father's unexpected words came so abruptly that Tommy missed their real meaning at first. Then sharp realization came. If Father left the church—an unheard-of event—the Staffords would have to leave the parsonage. They would have to leave Ulverston, too. How could Father preach if he didn't have a church?

"Very well, Thomas," Mother said in quiet determination. "Don't worry. God will find a way for you to preach His Word."

Celia interrupted in her impetuous way. "But, Father, why are you leaving the church? Don't you realize we will become beggars—paupers? The sheriff and the constables will hound us. If Squire Grantham is angry, he could throw us all in prison. Father, do you really know what you are doing—to yourself—to us?"

For once, Mother did not chide Celia for her quick tongue.

"Yes, Celia," Father said. "I do know what I am doing. I cannot continue to preach in a church whose sacraments, rituals, and ceremonies have become a hollow mockery of God."

"Then how are you going to worship God?" Celia asked.

"I don't know—I don't know." Father buried his face in his hands. "But I do know there is a direct way to God Himself."

Mother became excited. "Thomas, the man who is staying with the Fells at Swarthmoor Hall—he would help you see the light. You know the one I mean—George Fox."

"George Fox?" Father echoed in disgust. "Why, he's nothing but a street preacher. I would never seek help from a religious ranter like that. No, I must find my own path."

Celia, flushed and upset, began to argue. "But, Father, the squire will take the glebe lands away. How will we raise our food? What will we live on?"

Father looked stunned. It was plain that he had been thinking only of fulfilling God's will.

"Would your brother help?" Mother asked in a timid voice.

Father's face cleared. "Of course! I'd completely forgotten about the inheritance. My share of the rents seemed so small it didn't seem worthwhile making the trip to Devon each year, but if we had to, we could live on that income."

A knock on the door startled the whole family.

"It must be a parishioner," Mother said. "Poor Widow Buxby's down with the ague again, and with her son gone, it has been mighty hard running the inn alone—though I don't know how she could get any message to us if she did need help," she added.

A man called out, "Is this the home of Thomas Stafford, the parson?"

Mother opened the door. "Yes. Won't you come in?"

A stocky man entered and looked around with a calculating air at the thick, whitewashed walls, the oak furniture, and clean floors. "I'm the undersheriff. I understand you don't own this place."

"No," Father said. "It's part of the church living."

"You have any debts?"

"No."

The undersheriff cleared his throat. "I understand you had a talk with the squire today. He's much upset about your going. Says if you'll leave the cattle and farm implements, that'll square things up for running away like this. Says it's going to cost a pretty penny finding a new parson and bringing him here in time for the next service."

Father stammered in surprise. "Why, when I talked to the squire, he said everything could be arranged."

"That was before he had a gout attack," the under-

14

sheriff said. "I suppose you have wherewithal to live on?"

Father flushed. "We'll manage."

"I was going to say the squire would take it ill if you left a good church living and then became a burden to the county. He has no sympathy for heretics."

"But I'm not a heretic."

The undersheriff ignored Father's protest. "At any rate, the squire has given me my orders. The men are outside now, taking the movables—cattle, farm equipment, and the like."

Father slapped his open palm on the table. "The squire can't do this. The cattle and farm equipment are mine, my own property. They're not part of the church living."

The undersheriff did not look directly at anyone. He stared first at the beamed ceiling, and then at the small, latticed windows. "You'll have to leave everything, the squire says."

Somehow, the undersheriff's words were saying something else, something Tommy couldn't grasp, but dark and threatening.

"Very well," Father said. "It will take only a few days to move our furniture and household goods."

The undersheriff grinned in embarrassment, showing big, square, yellow teeth. "You don't need to worry about those items. The men will take care of them. We'll leave a two-wheeled cart for your clothes and personal things."

Mother gasped, and the undersheriff avoided her gaze. "I'm only following the squire's orders, ma'am. He don't hold much with heretics. After all, Parson

15

Stafford, here, has only himself to blame, excuse my saying so." He turned to Father. "Did anyone request you to leave the church, parson?"

"No," Father admitted. "Or rather, yes. God did."

The undersheriff blinked. "Oh, He did?" He cocked his head on one side. "I suppose you'll turn to street preaching now. Seems to be a lot of it in England these days. People are getting all stirred up by preachers like this George Fox, for instance. He's been raising a real riot around Ulverston. Folks are pretty upset because he denied the church. Well, I won't take up more of your time. I guess now that you're leaving, you're in a hurry to pack up and be on your way."

Mother forced a laugh. "We're not leaving just yet, not until we know where we're going."

The undersheriff hunched his shoulders, as if trying to shrug off an unpleasant weight. A sudden chill enveloped Tommy. Why didn't the man go? He'd said enough. But the undersheriff was not quite through.

"The squire gives you until sunup to vacate this place."

2

Stranger unto All

The door closed behind the undersheriff. Father motioned the family to sit down at the table.

"Elizabeth," he said to Mother, "I'm going to Devon and see about my inheritance. I'll start this very night."

"Oh, Thomas, no one is safe on the roads at night." Mother's voice tightened in alarm. "Widow Buxby says that lately there have been more highwaymen than ever."

Father laughed aloud. "I'm sure I will not provide any temptation for highwaymen." He stood up and took a deep breath. "I feel suddenly free. Now, help me pack a few clothes. One advantage of being poor," he added, "is that the burden is light. Oh, Elizabeth, in spite of all that's happened today, my heart is filled with joy. I feel that God has guided me into the right decision."

"But, Father, where will *we* go?" Celia's wail filled the little room.

"Why, why—" A bewildered look crossed Father's

17

face. Then he smiled. "You'll go stay at the inn. Mother can help Mrs. Buxby, and you children will make yourselves useful, I know. It shouldn't take me more than two weeks to go to Devon and back."

There was little sleep for the Stafford family after Father left that night. By dawn the two-wheeled cart had been packed. When it was time to start to the inn, Tommy and Celia took turns pulling the cart. The sun was well up when Tommy spotted the inn sign, a brilliant yellow lamb painted on a brown board.

At the gate, Tommy called, "Mrs. Buxby! Mrs. Buxby!"

In a moment the wide front door of the inn was flung open. A tall, thin woman hurried out, rubbing one shoulder. "Why, Mrs. Stafford! I declare! What on earth has happened?"

Mother explained, and added, "We'll pay you as soon as my husband returns. In the meantime, we'll be glad to help out with the work of the inn."

Mrs. Buxby kept shaking her head in disapproval. "I can use help, all right, but I don't know what good is going to come of all this. A parson can't just walk out of his church like that. He should have talked it over with some of the other parsons around here. Priest Lampitt would soon show him where his duty lies." Mrs. Buxby warmed up to her lecture. "What is your husband going to do? Has he taken up with some of those ranters who parade through the town barefoot and shrieking? I hear the doctor's serving man has become a ranter. Well, come in, come in." Mrs. Buxby sounded grudging. "I guess it's an act of Christian charity to take you in. Otherwise, you'd be paupers."

Tommy flinched. The word *pauper* struck at him like a poisonous snake. Everyone knew what paupers were—beggars in rags. He looked at Celia. Her face was white and pinched. He knew she felt as he did about charity.

Mother, with head held high, followed Mrs. Buxby into the inn without looking around.

"Celia," Tommy whispered, "do you think Father did right to leave the church?"

Celia batted back tears. "Yes, of course, but it's hard on us."

Tommy followed Celia inside to a narrow parlor with whitewashed walls and low ceiling with black oak beams. He stood by a rush-bottomed chair and stared at the unlit fireplace. Would Mrs. Buxby regret her charity? What if Father didn't get back when he planned? Or worse, what if he were robbed by highwaymen? Would Mrs. Buxby put them out? Would they have to wander from door to door begging their food?

For the first time in his life Tommy began to think about God. Who was He? Did He want His followers to be deprived of work, of clothing, of food, to follow Him? What did He offer in return? How could Father know what he was doing? What did it feel like to make a decision to follow God? Was God like a person, or was He a feeling inside a person? Tommy stared at the fireplace, unable to answer even one of the questions he had asked himself.

When Mrs. Buxby took the Staffords upstairs, Tommy looked into the guest rooms, large, comfortable, and inviting. He began to feel better, but Mrs. Buxby kept on going to the end of the hall where the roof sloped. She pointed out two tiny rooms with slanted ceilings, hardly more than closets.

"This ought to do," she said, folding her arms. Her tone added, "For the likes of you."

The Staffords unloaded the cart under Mrs. Buxby's prying gaze and disapproving sniffs. Celia looked like a thundercloud, but she held her tongue. Only Mother seemed able to accept the new life with calm and assurance.

Tommy was experiencing another first in his life— the shame felt by those who beg—and he did not like the feeling at all.

For the next few days Mrs. Buxby set the whole family to cleaning the inn. Nothing satisfied her. One morning Tommy inwardly rebelled. He was tired of hearing Mrs. Buxby complain, tired of scrubbing hearthstones, and he knew Celia was, too. All three of the Staffords had scrubbed, scoured, and dusted until the whole inn sparkled, but every day Mrs. Buxby whined in a droning voice, and today was no exception.

"As if the ague wasn't enough, my shoulder is just killing me. I can hear it grating." Her thin face lined with pain, Mrs. Buxby groaned and massaged her shoulder. "Mrs. Stafford! Oh, Mrs. Stafford! Where are you?"

Mother came in from the kitchen, a pleasant smile on her face. She slipped a book into her apron pocket.

Mrs. Buxby sniffed. "Hmmmm. Reading your Bible again. That won't pay your debts, and then you tell me you are going to market tomorrow. Is it to spend money you don't have?" Mrs. Buxby sank into a chair. "Please rub my back."

Mother massaged Mrs. Buxby's shoulders.

"My son Edward used to rub my back before he volunteered for the army." Mrs. Buxby began to cry. "Oh, my dear boy! Will I ever see him again?" In the same breath she added, "This morning I took a good dose of elixir and hung three spiders about my throat to drive the ague away. That'll do more good than reading the Bible." She wriggled and groaned. "I don't see why you insist on going to market tomorrow, but now that you aren't bringing me any more eggs, perhaps you could get some there."

"Of course," Mother said. "I'll be glad to." She kept on massaging.

"Mrs. Stafford, you could earn your living rubbing sick folks' backs. You'd never have to accept charity then."

Tommy ducked lower over his scrub brush. Rebellion surged through him. How could Mrs. Buxby call it charity when Mother, Celia, and he had worked so hard? It was a relief when Celia nudged him.

"I can't stand any more of Mrs. Buxby's charity," she whispered, her hazel eyes snapping. "When we go to market tomorrow, I'm going to get myself hired out and work for some rich family. Mother told me months ago that I could try. After all, I'm fourteen. It's time I earned my own living."

Tommy agreed, but a miserable ache went through him. Why did he have to be just twelve?

"It's too bad you can't get a job, too," Celia went on. "You're tall and strong for your age. Being blond makes you seem older, and you have pretty good sense, too."

Praise from Celia was rare. Tommy felt better.

21

"Will you help me pack my belongings later?" Celia asked. "If I get hired out tomorrow, I'm not coming back here."

Tommy agreed to help.

At the other side of the room Mrs. Buxby stood up. "There, Mrs. Stafford, that'll do, thank you."

"Then I'll start the bread, Mrs. Buxby." Mother went down the long hallway into the kitchen.

"Young master over there had better stir his lazy bones and clean out the stable and the close," Mrs. Buxby said, her voice filled with sarcasm. "Do you think I'm letting you people go to market tomorrow without a fair share of work today?"

Tears of defiance stung Tommy's eyelids. He hurried to the kitchen and told Mother what Mrs. Buxby had said. "Why does she say such things, Mother?" he asked.

Mother ladled out flour. "She has the ague, and that makes tempers short. You must be patient, Tommy."

"But nothing we do satisfies her. Do we have to stay here?"

"Yes, until Father returns. If we didn't, we'd have to live on charity."

That word again. Tommy went out to the stable almost bursting with anger. He made a sudden resolve. Tomorrow at the market he too would try to get a job. Many times rich country gentlemen came to market to trade or sell with other landowners. He could surely find a job with someone.

Stimulated by his resolve, Tommy jerked the feed too fast from the bin. It scattered over the dirt floor. Dismayed at his carelessness, Tommy brushed up the feed from the shadowy corners with special care. Feed was expensive, Mrs. Buxby had kept repeating. Guests expected the best.

A penetrating call interrupted his thoughts.

"Tommy! Tom-meee!"

"I'm coming," he shouted. He ran through the kitchen where Mother kneaded bread dough. Panting, and expecting to hear Celia call again, Tommy reached the entrance hall. Celia flounced down the broad stairway. Her red petticoat flashed from under her gray dress.

"My packing's all done, Tommy," she said. "No thanks to you." Now she acted like her usual spirited self.

A loud wail from Mrs. Buxby silenced them both. Mother ran in from the kitchen, holding her flour-covered hands away from her clothes. "Mrs. Buxby, whatever is the matter? Do compose yourself."

Mrs. Buxby looked mournfully at the fireplace. Her sharp chin quivered. "I can't help it. I just saw some soldiers go by. When I think of something happening to my own precious soldier boy, my breath just chokes in my throat. I don't feel so well. I think you'd better not go to market tomorrow. I need you here."

Mother's eyes had a faraway look. "Oh, I wouldn't miss the market for anything."

Mrs. Buxby folded her arms. "Now, Mrs. Stafford, I know why you're going. You hope to see that peculiar preaching man you told me about, the one going afoot all over the country. The man with the funny name—Wolf, isn't it?"

Mother smiled. "It's Fox, George Fox." Her cheeks

glowed. "He's led hundreds all over England to the light of God."

Mrs. Buxby pursed her lips. "But isn't it odd—him wandering around the country, getting people all stirred up? I'm sure the priests in Ulverston don't approve. I know Priest Lampitt would tell him a thing or two, and your own husband would too—unless—unless—" Her eyes widened. "Is that why your husband left his church?"

"No," Mother said.

Tommy saw suspicion in Mrs. Buxby's eyes.

"This man's followers," Mrs. Buxby went on, "don't they call them *shakers?*"

"Quakers," Mother said. "Or, rather, Friends."

"Well, this man Fox sounds like one of them nasty bugs to me."

Mother looked puzzled. "Like what?"

"That horrible bug—you know, a tick—a hairy tick."

Tommy and Celia burst into laughter. After a moment Mother joined in.

"Mrs. Buxby, you are priceless," she said. "You mean a *heretic*. No," she went on in a thoughtful tone, "he is not a heretic."

"Is he going to be in these parts soon?"

"He's already here. He's staying at Margaret Fell's place."

Mrs. Buxby's eyes rounded in surprise. "Margaret Fell—Judge Fell's wife? She, the mother of all those children?"

"The same. She has been helping George Fox with circular letters to his followers, so I've heard." Mother started to the kitchen. "I'd better get back to the bread."

From outside the inn came the sound of men's voices, high-pitched in anger. Mrs. Buxby opened the front door. Tommy and Celia crowded behind her. A group of men jostled a big man dressed in an unusual suit made of leather. Someone tried to knock off the stranger's white, broad-brimmed hat. The big man made no move to defend himself, but allowed the others to push him down the road.

"They're running him out of town," Celia cried out. "Poor man! What has he done?"

Tommy could see that the man was not of the gentry. He looked like a common farmer, but his face had a kind, patient expression. His eyes were blue, alive, and compelling. The man's very presence quickened the air with something mysterious and urgent. A wiry, dark-haired man darted about shouting to the crowd.

"Why, that's William Lampitt, I declare," Mrs. Buxby exclaimed. "Why is he carrying on like that? He should be in his church if he wants to make a spectacle of himself."

"What come you hither for?" someone shouted to the stranger.

"What have you to say?" others called.

Still another added in irritation, "From whence came you?"

"From the Lord," the stranger answered, "and seeing there are so many questions asked, I will answer them."

"We have heard enough of his answers already," a man rudely interrupted. "Let us round up our learned men to dispute him."

"Priest Lampitt! Priest Lampitt!" several called.

25

The stranger's deep voice rang out. "I came not to dispute but to declare the way of salvation and the way of everlasting life."

"Let us hear Priest Lampitt!"

The wiry priest held up his hands to silence the group, but the stranger spoke first. "I have something to speak to the people. Thou," he told the priest, "carried thyself foolishly the other day and spakest against thy conscience and reason."

"No, no, I did not." Priest Lampitt's face darkened with anger. "What are you trying to do here in Ulverston?"

"Preach repentance to the people."

There was an uproar from the men clustered around. Some began throwing clods and stones. Then a new voice broke in. "I charge you all to keep peace in the name of the commonwealth."

"It's the constable," Mrs. Buxby exclaimed. "Oh, look! He's been hit on the head. The blood is pouring down his face."

At the sight of blood, the men, including Priest Lampitt, slunk away. The stranger helped the constable to the inn door.

"What canst thou do for him?" he asked Mrs. Buxby.

"*Thou?*" she snapped. "Why do you *thou* me?" She called Mother, who took the constable inside.

Mrs. Buxby stared at the stranger's white hat, as if waiting for him to take it off. He made no move to do so.

"Haven't you common courtesy enough to take off your hat?" she asked.

"Doth this trouble thee?" The stranger took off his

hat and put it on again, without a hint of arrogance.

"*Thee*?" Mrs. Buxby drew herself up. "Such insolence I never heard. Why do you *thee* and *thou* me? You are no higher rank in the world than I am."[*]

Celia appealed to the big man. "Won't you take off your hat?"

"When the Lord sent me forth into the world, He forbade me to put off my hat to any, high or low," he said. "It's an honor invented by man."

Mrs. Buxby shrank back. "Why, he's out of his head," she whispered to Tommy. When the man did not move, she demanded, "Who are you?"

"A stranger unto all," he replied.

At these words Mrs. Buxby flapped her apron. "Get out. Don't ever come here again," she shouted, her cheeks mottled with rage.

The stranger turned without a word and started toward the road. A little later the constable left, his head bandaged by Mother's deft fingers. Tommy went to the kitchen and told Mother the whole incident. "And Mrs. Buxby sent him away," he concluded.

Mother sank down on a stool. "But, Tommy, that's the man I want to talk to. I just know he could help your father."

Tommy stared at her in consternation. The scene at the Ulverston market flashed through his mind—Quaker—Friends—*thee* and *thou*—never lift their hats to people. How could he have been so stupid as not to recognize the man at once?

"Oh, Mother, that was George Fox himself, wasn't it?" He ran to the door. "I'll go and bring him back."

---

[*]*Thee* and *thou* were forms of speech used for servants and anyone beneath one's social class in England in 1652.

Tommy dashed outside and ran down the road in the direction George Fox had taken. But as he ran, a frightening thought struck him. If he brought Fox back against Mrs. Buxby's orders, she would turn Mother, Celia, and himself out of the inn. Without money, they would have no place to go. Could George Fox really help Father?

Far ahead Tommy could see Fox walking toward Swarthmoor Hall. *Shall I overtake him or let him go?* Tormented with indecision, Tommy slowed his steps, not ready to turn back to the inn, and even less ready to overtake Fox. At the edge of the heath five or six men sprang from the bushes and with shouts and jeers surrounded George Fox.

"Run him out of Ulverston! He has bewitched the people! Reverend Lampitt said so!" Tommy heard someone call. The men rained blows on Fox's head, shoulders, and back. Tommy watched in horror. There was nothing he could do to help. If only he had caught up with Fox sooner, they might both have been back at the inn and the ambush prevented.

But it was too late now.

3

Man of Faith

Trembling, yet fascinated, Tommy watched George Fox push his way toward Swarthmoor Hall disregarding the blows of the shouting men. If someone pushed him down, he rose. If others plucked at his coat, he worked himself free with a slow, relentless purposefulness. One by one the men dropped away until at last Fox walked alone.

Tommy let his breath out in a vast sigh of relief. What did this man have that enabled him to overpower his enemies without exchanging blow for blow? All the way back to the inn, Tommy marveled at what he had seen.

In the kitchen he found Mother, Mrs. Buxby, and Celia.

"I declare," Mrs. Buxby said, "I've never seen the likes. Mrs. Stafford, you should have seen that horrible man. No wonder he was being run out of town."

"That was George Fox, Mrs. Buxby," Mother said in a low voice.

Mrs. Buxby tossed her head. "I don't care who he

29

is. He's not setting foot in my inn. Why, he wasn't even civil. '*Thou*,' he says to me, him no higher rank than I am. 'Thou me, *thou* my dog,' say I. Let him come back here and '*thou*' me and I'll '*thou*' his teeth down his throat." Her chin jutted in such a forbidding way that she reminded Tommy of a bulldog. In spite of his concern, he grinned at Celia.

"Now, Mrs. Buxby," Mother said, "he is a man of faith. I know he has a good reason, based on the Bible, for everything he does."

"For rousing up honest folk the way he did to-day?" Mrs. Buxby all but screamed. "Is this what he does all over England? Mrs. Stafford, you'd better think twice about listening to such a man."

Mrs. Buxby's warnings continued throughout the next week. "He's bewitched everyone at Swarthmoor Hall. Reverend Lampitt said so," she announced in triumph the next market day. "I don't suppose you'll be wanting to go to market now, will you?"

"Yes, we're planning to," Mother said.

An odd expression crossed Mrs. Buxby's thin face. She held up her hand. "Listen—do you hear horses?"

They listened for a minute, and Tommy burst out in vexation. "Oh, Mother, if there are guests, that'll spoil everything." He gasped. "I mean—" He did not dare say he hoped to get a job that day. He and Celia had kept their secret all week long. Once more, Celia had her bundle ready for the job she hoped to get. "I mean, we'll be late going to the market if there are guests," he added lamely.

"It's too early for guests to come and stay all night, isn't it, Mrs. Buxby?" Celia asked. "Maybe they just want something to eat."

Tommy felt comforted. Celia sounded so certain.

Mrs. Buxby's eyes narrowed. "Maybe it's that there George Wolf and all those friends he's rounding up."

"Fox, Mrs. Buxby. His name is George Fox," Mother said.

"No matter. He ought to be thrown in prison. I wonder that Judge Fell allows him at Swarthmoor. Of course he's gone so much on his circuit, he probably doesn't realize what's going on in his own house." She stopped talking and listened. "Whoever's out there on horseback has arrived. Tommy, take the horses to the close."

Tommy ran outside. Two men, bulky in their traveling coats, knee-high, flared boots, and big feathered hats, dismounted. Both men sagged at each step as if exhausted.

The taller one quickened his pace and came toward the doorway where Mrs. Buxby fingered her skirt, ready to curtsy. The man was young, Tommy could see, and good-looking.

"Good day to you. We saw the Golden Lamb," the young man said, nodding toward the wooden sign overhead, "and we knew that no harm would befall us here." He flashed a smile toward Mrs. Buxby and bowed. Her stern face softened, and she purred a welcome.

The shorter of the two men stood behind the other, holding his head to one side in a peculiar way. A green and red plaid cloth, wrapped like a one-sided bandage over one ear, slipped a little. The man adjusted it with a quick movement. At a nudge from his companion, he removed his feathered hat with care and made a jerky bow.

31

"Come in, come in," Mrs. Buxby said.

The handsome man peered into the entrance hall. "And where is the host today?"

Mrs. Buxby's face twitched. "There is no host. I'm a widow. My only son volunteered for the army a year ago." She dabbed at her eyes with the corner of her apron.

"Oh, I see." The tall man paused and glanced at his companion, who exhaled in a grunt.

"No men here, then?" Both men glanced toward Tommy, then away, as if to dismiss him.

Tommy wriggled in discomfort. Why were they so interested about the host?

"We'll stay." With a motion for Tommy to tend to their horses, the men followed Mrs. Buxby inside.

Tommy led the horses past the close into the stable, feeling more troubled at every step. Something was wrong. In the first place, the horses were winded. Why would anyone ride horses that hard in the daytime unless there was an urgent reason? And why had the short man wrapped his head in the plaid scarf. It was only July. The weather was too mild for that much headgear.

"Maybe he has an earache," Tommy said to himself. He groomed the horses until their sides gleamed. Why had guests come today of all days? Maybe they wanted to go to market. After all, many people came into Ulverston on market day.

When he went back to the inn, Mrs. Buxby was all smiles. Her spry step astonished Tommy.

"They're real gentlemen." She whisked upstairs with a blue pitcher and two thick mugs.

Tommy went to the dining room, expecting to find

Celia setting the table for lunch. She wasn't there. He found her in the kitchen preparing a tray of food.

"What's happening? Where's Mother?" Tommy asked.

Celia spread a white napkin over the food. "Those men are pumping her and Mrs. Buxby about this county, the river, the roads, and all the big estates like Swarthmoor Hall and Squire Grantham's place. Mrs. Buxby is eating up all the attention. The handsome one keeps making sweeping bows and flourishing his hat."

She acted out her words, and Tommy grinned. "Mrs. Buxby thinks they're real gentlemen, Tommy, but I don't. There's something odd about them. They want their lunch upstairs, and then they are going to sleep."

"Sleep? In the daytime?" Tommy's astonishment must have touched off a response in Celia. Her hazel eyes danced.

"Yes, in the daytime, and do you want to know a secret?"

"Celia, what is it? Please tell me." Tommy was annoyed at himself for begging, but he had suspicions he couldn't put his finger on. Maybe Celia knew.

But Celia turned on her mischievous self. She twirled. Her red petticoat flashed from under her gray dress. She stepped out on tiptoe, her yellow stockings and cork slippers moving so fast they became a blur of color.

"I know a secret! I know a secret!"

Stung to fury, Tommy chased her halfway up the stairs. Celia whirled with her finger to her lips and pointed to the guest room.

33

2

"I know a secret, too, Celia." Tommy's voice came out in a hiss. "I saw their horses."

"What about them?"

"They're winded."

"Then that proves it."

"Proves what?"

"They're trying to hide. They're highwaymen."

The words struck Tommy like a whip. "You mean real highwaymen like Black Bart and people like that?" Tommy's mind swam with stories he had heard about Black Bart jumping from bushes onto people's coaches and robbing them, all the time smiling and using soft talk. No one in England dared travel at night without risking his life. Highwaymen terrorized the country.

"Yes, that's what I mean," Celia said, "and I know something even worse." She tapped the side of her head. "The shorter one doesn't have an ear. I saw." She shuddered. "His plaid scarf slipped. And you know what *that* means." She tapped her ear.

"You mean he's been in prison—and they punished him that way?"

Celia nodded. "It isn't unusual, you know, for that kind of people."

"But, Celia, what if they decide to *murder us?*" The words *murder us* came out half bleat, half shriek.

The horrible thought stayed with Tommy until afternoon. A shout sounded from upstairs, sending a quiver all through him.

"Boy! Boy!"

Taking two steps at a time, Tommy sped to the guest room and opened the door. "Yes, sir," he gasped.

A snarl of rage from the short man was the reply. He was sitting on the bed, with a big leather pouch near him. He crammed a pile of coins out of sight.

"Don't you have sense enough to knock before you come into a room?" The short man's face had turned an ugly dark red.

The handsome man shrugged. "No harm done. Boy, get our horses ready."

"Don't stand there staring like a booby," the short man snapped. "Get the horses."

Tommy gulped. "Yes, sir." He started out.

"Well, Bart," he heard the short man say, "I only hope the boy isn't too sharp."

Bart? Could this be Black Bart himself? Tommy's knees felt like water. He clung to the banister going downstairs and looked desperately around for Celia to tell her, but she wasn't in sight, and he did not dare stop before he got the horses ready.

When the men rode off, the Staffords, over Mrs. Buxby's protests, set out for the Ulverston market. Tommy sensed Mother's heartfelt hope that George Fox would be talking to the people there.

The market square overflowed with people laughing and talking. Fruit women with white aprons screamed their wares from market stalls. Carters fought for right-of-way for their carts to load and unload farm produce. Someone knocked over a crock of cream, and a woman wailed at the river of thick cream running over the cobblestones.

Near the square itself, a crowd of people pressed near a man who stood on a stone. There was no mistaking the big man in the leather suit and white hat.

"Mother, there he is!" Tommy exclaimed.

With an exclamation of joy, Mother hurried closer, with Tommy and Celia close behind. This time, there was no noise or movement from the people. No one spoke. Minutes passed. The big man in the broad-brimmed white hat stood as if waiting. Tommy felt a warm glow all over his body. A wave of indescribable, invigorating heat swept over him. It entered his feet and pushed upward until he tingled from head to foot.

"Come off from the world's ways. Be bold; be for the truth." George Fox's first words stirred the crowd.

"Come to the church," a man called. "Don't preach here on the street."

George Fox shook his head.

"It is something strange that he will not go into the house of God," the man said to his neighbor. "If he is a man of faith, why doesn't he prove it?"

Another called out, "George, why won't you go to the church?"

"Because God is not in a steeple house, a building made of wood and stone. He does not dwell in temples made with hands."

Some of the listeners murmured.

"Temples and churches are holy ground," a man shouted.

"No, they are not," Fox said. "Christ's church is made of living members. It is a spiritual household, which Christ is head of. He is not the head of an old building made up of lime, stones, and wood. It is your bodies that are the temples of God. He dwells within you."

Exclamations of astonishment and dismay rose from the crowd.

Someone near Tommy spoke in a low voice, "I am afraid of this man who goes after new lights."

A man in servant's livery of lavender and black pushed his way toward Fox. People drew back from the tall, lean man whose caved-in cheeks, inflamed by eruptions, glowed red. "It's Nick Hogan, the doctor's servant," Tommy heard someone say.

"I saw a vision of you," Nick Hogan said, partly to George Fox, partly to the crowd. "You were sitting in a great chair and I was to come and bow."

"Thou art but a beast." George Fox's stern reprimand quieted everyone. "This vision was a figure of thyself. Repent."

"You are jealous to say so." Nick clenched his fists. His shrill voice made unpleasant shivers go down Tommy's back. "I was told by God to come, and you are jealous of me because I have more of God's power than you."

"Leave this place." Fox stretched out his arm in a commanding gesture. "Thou art a false prophet."

Nick Hogan gulped and fled.

"Let this be a warning," Fox told the crowd. "False prophets have already come. True prophets bear fruit. Watch for that fruit." He continued. "Turn ye from darkness to light. Be led to truth. The light of Christ enlightens every man who comes into the world. Let Christ be thy teacher. He dwells within you."

Tommy listened to the strange words. How could Christ dwell within? In what way would He teach? How could a person be sure what was true and what was false, like Nick Hogan's ranting? Tommy determined to listen to George Fox every chance he got and find out the answer.

Later, at the inn, several quietly dressed people came and asked for rooms. "We were invited to stay at Swarthmoor Hall," they explained, "but there are so many Friends there already, Margaret Fell sent us here."

At first Mrs. Buxby stammered a reply. Tommy could see she was torn between gratitude at Mrs. Fell's thoughtfulness and getting mixed up with George Fox's Friends. After a moment's hesitation, she added a shilling to the usual rate of the rooms, and, with the money paid in advance, she nodded to Celia to show the Friends upstairs.

"There's a meeting at St. Mary's church," Celia told Mother and Tommy afterward. "It's tomorrow, and they hope George Fox will be there."

Over the protests of Mrs. Buxby, the Staffords went to church the next day with the Friends.

Reverend Lampitt blustered on for a long time in the crowded church. Then George Fox rose from among the Friends and went to the front of the church near Reverend Lampitt. As he turned to speak, a man caught him by the hand.

Someone near Tommy murmured, "That's John Sawrey, the justice."

"Do you want to speak?" Tommy heard the justice ask.

"Yes."

"You must speak according to the Scriptures, then," Justice Sawrey said.

"I will, and I have brought the Scriptures to prove what I have to say. I have some things to speak to Priest Lampitt and all of them." Fox took out his Bible from a coat pocket.

"You shall not speak!" Justice Sawrey cried.

A group of rude people in the front pews roared out, "Give him us! Give him us!"

The words touched off an uproar in the church. People plunged down the aisle and with staves, fists, and books fell upon George Fox. They knocked him down, kicked him, and trampled upon him. In the scramble, other people were tumbled about or knocked down. The Friends did not fight back but merely protected their heads from the blows.

At last Justice Sawrey called out, "Give him me!" He led Fox outside and put him into the hands of four officers. Tommy, coming out of the church with the others, heard the loud command: "Whip him and put him out of town!"

Two officers grabbed Fox by his arms and shoulders, another by his collar, and still another by his hands. They dragged him through mire and water toward the edge of town. Many friendly people who had come to market and then to the steeple house to hear Fox were knocked down. Several men threw George Fell, the judge's son, a boy about Tommy's age, into a ditch full of water. "Knock out the teeth of his head!" he heard a man shout.

At the edge of Ulverston, the officers turned back, as if they had done their duty. Then the mob took over. They grabbed hedge stakes, holm bushes, and willows to use as whips and beat Fox, thrusting him among the other people. They in turn fell on him with clubs and staves and struck him repeatedly on the head, arms, and shoulders.

A sudden quiet came over everyone. The big man had sagged to the ground.

Celia, with tears streaming down her face, sobbed, "They've killed him."

Tommy fought with himself to hold back his own tears. Why would people kill a man who came to tell them about Christ, their inward teacher? Why? Why? Why?

4

Follow the Leader

George Fox lay still. Then to the astonishment of everyone, he rose, stretched out his arms, and cried out in a loud voice, "Strike again. Here are my arms and my head and my cheeks."

A mason standing near Fox suddenly brought his rule-staff across Fox's hand and arm so hard that the skin was struck off. Many exclaimed in horror. "He'll never have the use of his hand again," they said. But George Fox looked at his bloody, outstretched hand, and in the sight of all, he recovered the use of his hand and arm.

The crowd began to quarrel among themselves. Some claimed a miracle. Others threatened Fox. "If you come to town again, we will kill you," a man called.

On hearing this threat, Fox started toward the Ulverston market. The Staffords followed. Tommy felt as if he could not bear to lose sight of the big man. He knew Mother and Celia felt the same.

On the way, a soldier with drawn sword ran up to

Fox. "Sir," Tommy heard him say, "I am your servant. I am ashamed that you should be thus abused, for you are a man. I'll assist you." He waved his sword.

George Fox caught the soldier's sword hand. "It is no matter. The Lord's power is over all. Put up thy sword if thou wilt go with me."

Fox started toward Swarthmoor, about a mile south of Ulverston. The Staffords, along with others, followed him. A coach drove up, and a plump, nervous little woman jumped out unassisted. "Oh, Mr. Fox, I understand the Friends are holding their meetings at Swarthmoor. But will you come to our place and have a meeting? We have a large estate—I'm Squire Grantham's wife. Please have a meeting there tomorrow."

She clasped her hands in entreaty. "I have an invalid son—our only child—and I believe he can be divinely healed."

George Fox promised to come the next day, and went on toward Swarthmoor. To Tommy's consternation, Mrs. Grantham burst into tears. Both Mother and Celia sprang to comfort her. "It's because I'm so happy," the squire's wife explained. She dropped forward and would have fallen, but Celia caught her. "Thank you, my dear. What a deft touch you have!" She looked at Mother. "Are you a Friend?"

"Not yet, but I hope to be."

The little woman beamed. "That's just the position I'm in. Won't you come to the meeting? And your children, too, of course. What is your name?"

"We are the Staffords," Mother said. "This is Tommy and Celia."

At the name *Stafford,* the plump little woman reddened. "Are you the pastor's wife?"

"Yes."

At first Mrs. Grantham shrank back. Then understanding dawned on her face. "Oh, is your husband a Friend? Is that why he left the church?"

Mother smiled a little sadly. "No, it wasn't for that reason. In fact, he refuses to hear George Fox." She added, "He isn't here now. He's gone to Devon."

The other woman looked searchingly into Mother's face. "My husband said your family deserved to become paupers. That's a very harsh judgment." She hesitated. "Are you looking for work?"

"No. I'm helping Mrs. Buxby at the inn. We'll get along all right."

"Oh, Mother," Celia said in reproach, "*I'm* looking for work."

"Then, my dear, you shall have a place in my household. You can help me with Dirk, my son. Would you like that?"

"Oh, yes." Celia jumped in joy.

"First come to the meeting tomorrow," Mrs. Grantham said. "Oh, if George Fox can help my son, I'll feel as if—as if I'd been let out of prison. You know he had been in prison, don't you?"

"No," Mother said.

"Yes, in Nottingham. I believe it was in 1649, and then again in Derby two years ago. One of the Friends told me, but he said George Fox didn't seem to mind, and kept saying that Christ had the key. Isn't that beautiful? As soon as he came to Ulverston, I determined this time I would talk with him, no matter what my husband said."

Mrs. Grantham turned to her coach with a wave of her hand.

The next day the Staffords came to the squire's estate. Mrs. Grantham met George Fox and the Friends at the gatehouse and led them down a wide walk bordered with red and purple flowers. Neat green hedges, ash and sycamore trees, and a fountain in the garden made Tommy and Celia gasp. The great house that rose at the end of the walk seemed to grow as they approached. At the entrance hall, Mrs. Grantham stopped until everyone had crowded in. "The squire's in the reception room." She nodded toward closed double doors.

The Friends, to make room, backed down a narrow, dark corridor. Tommy, moving backward, heard heavy breathing behind him. He turned and made out a figure sitting in a hunched position on a large, carved chest. The man muttered and drummed his heels against the sides. Tommy saw the lavender and black livery. There was no mistaking the man—Nick Hogan. With a burst of invective under his breath, Nick wriggled through the Friends past Mrs. Grantham.

"Why, Nick," she called, "where have you been? Dr. Huber expected you to be here."

Nick ducked and hurried on.

"Poor Nick," Mrs. Grantham said. "He's probably been ranting on the streets again. I don't know why Dr. Huber keeps him." She went to George Fox. "Oh, sir, I'm afraid you can't see my son, after all. He refuses to see anyone. I'm afraid he's a bit spoiled, poor invalid boy." She stood up on tiptoe. "Now, if everyone will wait here, I'll see how my husband is. Dr. Huber is with him. The squire has been having terrible gout attacks, but I'm sure everything will be all right for our meeting." She stood by the double doors and listened.

Someone pushed Tommy aside. Startled, he turned, half expecting to see Nick Hogan again. But it was a man in green and gold livery.

"What are you people doing here?" the man asked in a haughty tone. "Move along, there, move along. If you want work, come around to the kitchen entrance."

Mrs. Grantham checked him. "Why, Padgett! These are my friends. I told you about them earlier."

"Oh, madam, pray pardon me." Prim disapproval showed on Padgett's sallow face, but he bowed almost to the floor.

Celia nudged Tommy. "He must be used to seeing people in silks and satins instead of plain clothes," she whispered.

Padgett cast an anxious glance toward the closed double doors, as much as to say, "Whatever will the squire think?" He bowed himself down the corridor. At the chest he looked startled and fingered a huge padlock dangling from the lid. Clucking as if satisfied that it was secured, he disappeared into the kitchen area.

"He must be the steward," Mother said. "All big estates have one."

From behind the double doors a man's voice rose in wrath, accompanied by resounding thumps of what sounded like a heavy stick.

"Dr. Huber, you have a fine carriage, which I help pay for; you have a man in livery; you carry your sword like a gentleman born; you charge your one

46

shilling a mile. You've blooded me, vomited me, purged me, blistered me, cupped me to a fare-you-well. I say cure me, or get out."

A door slammed. A portly short man came out, breathing heavily. He shook down his lace cuffs and straightened his sword in an angry gesture. Then his glance fell on Nick Hogan.

"My lord," Nick said, his face alternately flushing and paling, "the man in leathern breeches is come."

The doctor ignored the remark. "Where have you been, Nick? You knew I was to attend Squire Grantham today. He tells me you've become a religious ranter. You've been with me many years, but this is too much. I hired you to serve me, not to rant in the streets. You're fired."

Nick shrank back. His lips twitched. "The squire put you up to this. 'I'll have my revenge,' saith the Lord. The squire has lost his soul. His gold will do him no good either." Nick rubbed his palms together. A trickle of saliva dribbled from the corners of his mouth. Once again, he ran off.

The doctor sighed and wiped his brow with a trembling hand. "Well, sir," he said, singling out George Fox, "so you're the one people have been talking about. Why don't you go in and cure the squire? My medicine hasn't helped." He did not sound sarcastic, Tommy noted, but almost matter-of-fact.

From inside, a voice roared out. "Who are these people, Amy? Some more of your nonsense? George Fox is with them? Well, let him in. He can't be any worse than that nincompoop of a doctor. Maybe he can take my mind off my foot. All right, don't stand

47

there all day. Show him in. Show them all in."

For a moment, Tommy felt frightened. Would the squire recognize the Stafford family? No, he decided. The squire had never spoken to anyone except Father.

Tommy followed the others into a vast room, the largest he had ever seen. Frescoes and carved designs covered walls and ceiling. Squire Grantham sat in an ornate chair upholstered in green velvet, with his swollen foot resting on a purple, tufted stool studded with gilt nails.

George Fox stepped ahead. "Peace be with this house." The rich tones filled the big room.

"So you're George Fox."

"I am."

"I'm Squire Grantham."

Fox did not move.

The squire exploded. "Well! Don't you realize who I am? Take off your hat, man, in the presence of your superior."

"I cannot."

"Cannot?" Astonishment and rage showed on Squire Grantham's broad face. He puffed and snorted. Then curiosity seemed to overcome him. "Do you have a head injury?"

"No."

"Then why won't you take off your hat? Do you want people to think you're insane—like those wretches at Bedlam I see on my trips to London? What's wrong with taking off your hat?"

"It is an honor invented by man," George Fox said. "Christ saith, 'How can ye believe, who receive honor of one another and seek not the honor that

48

cometh from God only?" Christ receives not honor of men." The syllables rolled out in forceful waves from the big, ungainly man.

The squire sucked in his breath. "I have no strength to dispute with you. My gout hurts too much. Keep your hat on, if you insist."

"May we have our meeting?" Mrs. Grantham reminded her husband.

"In a minute, in a minute," the squire growled. "I understand you Quakers are a plain people," he said to George Fox. "I'm glad to hear it. I've saved a fortune already now that my wife has done away with her false curls, her powders, patches, and fine clothes. She doesn't even wear jewelry anymore. I've had to put it in the big chest in the hall for safekeeping, and one of these days I'll exchange it for gold coin. There'd be enough to run this estate for a year. So all in all, I'm really rather grateful to you Friends, even though I don't subscribe to your beliefs."

"Everyone is waiting," Mrs. Grantham murmured.

"Have your meeting then. Use the private chapel."

George Fox shook his head.

"What's the matter with a chapel?" the squire demanded. "It's a church. Isn't that holy ground?"

"God's people are His holy ground," Fox said.

For a moment the squire remained speechless. "So now you deny the church. You are a strange man, Mr. Fox. How the Church of England tolerates you, I don't know. I wonder how our protector, Oliver Cromwell, would regard your views."

"I have talked to him. He is in some ways a God-fearing man, but his days are numbered," Fox said.

"Cromwell's days are numbered?" The squire sat

49

back in astonishment. "Are you a prophet, too? I wish you could prophesy about my invalid son, poor, weakly, puny thing." He sighed. "But enough. Go have your meeting—in the small drawing room, if you disdain the chapel."

Padgett entered with stiff dignity, followed by an old coachman. Padgett spoke to the squire in low tones. The squire clumped his stick on the floor.

"That's what happens every year at this time—another volunteer for the army muster. Now my sheepherder's gone. Any of you Friends want a job?" He looked over the group and stopped when he saw Tommy. "Here's a likely-looking lad. You're too young for the army and for all this religious talk coming up, too, I'll wager. Would you like to herd my sheep?"

Tommy felt a big grin spread over his face. He turned to Mother. "Oh, may I, Mother? I know about sheep. They always follow a leader. It's simple."

Mother stammered, "Why, I never thought—"

The squire interrupted. "Don't let them in my prize herbs, that's all I ask. I'm taking the last of them to the fair tomorrow. I've won the prize three years straight, now. Old John will take care of you." Padgett ushered Tommy and the coachman out of the reception room. Once outside Padgett disappeared.

Old John led Tommy to the back yard, a small town in itself, with blacksmith shop, carpentry shop, dairy, cattle sheds, and other small buildings. Old John found a shepherd's crook twice as long as Tommy, and let the sheep out of the fold.

"Mind, now, let them browse over the meadow, and don't let them jump over that low stone wall and nibble master's herbs."

50

Tommy did not know whether to carry the staff the long way like a lance, or straight over his head. When the ewes tumbled over each other to follow the leader, Tommy slid the smooth shank through his hands, circled an old ewe's neck, and tugged. She ignored the crook. Sheep began to press on Tommy from all sides, in a slow, relentless pressure. Tommy almost fell over his own feet. The squeezing intensified, and Tommy tried to turn back to call Old John to help but the coachman had already disappeared.

There was nothing to do but yield to the rippling movement and move with the sheep. They poured through the gate to the road and then scattered over the meadow. Tommy laughed in relief when he found he had room to walk. He reached the crook to the sky, exulting in his new job and marveling how he and Celia would be working in the same household.

The afternoon sun warmed him. The grassy fields never looked greener. A sense of power swelled in Tommy. The afternoon passed away.

When it was time to turn the sheep back, Tommy prodded the leader. "I can control you—you old mutton head," he said. He maneuvered the leader from the low stone wall bordering the squire's prize herbs.

The sound of horses' hooves startled him. Six perfectly matched gray horses brought a coach down the road. Tommy stared at the elegant contraption. From the high front seat, Old John drove the horses. Tommy waved, but Old John looked stern. He motioned with his whip.

"Get those sheep out of the way." He acted as if he had never seen Tommy before.

"Yes, sir." Tommy had forgotten about the sheep for the moment. As the coach passed, he discovered to his horror that the leader had squeezed through a hole in the fence where a stone had been dislodged. The squire's prize herb garden! Tommy choked with panic. He threw out the crook and tugged, but nothing stopped the sheep. They crushed themselves close to the fence. Some tried to jump over. Tears of indignation and helplessness poured down Tommy's face. He was going to lose his job the very first day.

5

Family Disgrace

The sheep piled on top of each other. Tommy hooked
and clawed in desperation, only to feel the crook dis-
lodge again and again from the slippery, wriggling
creatures. To make matters worse, he saw George
Fox coming down the road from the manor house.
Fox read from an open book. Even from a distance,
Tommy recognized the Bible.

Tommy struggled on, choking from the cloud of
dust rising from the road. He did not dare look up
again, but he became aware of a new and different
movement. A harmonious rippling eased through the
mass of surging sheep. The full-bodied voice of
George Fox rose above the turmoil. For all his big-
ness, Fox eased himself through to the hole in the
fence, dislodged the leader of the sheep, and heaved
it bodily into the road. The other sheep turned and
followed, bleating and desperate. Tommy sagged with
relief. The squire's herbs were safe.

"Are you a shepherd?" Tommy asked after he
had thanked George Fox.

"Christ is the true shepherd that laid down His life for His sheep, and His sheep heard His voice and followed Him." Fox leaned down to pat a ewe going past.

Tommy tried to figure out the double meaning he sensed in Fox's words. They seemed somehow directed to him. The big man's intense blue eyes had lit up with hidden fire. Tommy began to fill up the gap in the wall with loose stones. George Fox tucked his Bible more securely in his pocket and helped. Together they heaved and tugged at the stones.

A rumble far down the road made them both straighten. The squire's coach was coming back. When the coach reached the gap, Tommy heard a boyish voice call out a command.

"John! Stop the coach!" The order came again. "Old John! Stop, I say!"

A pale young boy looked out of the coach window. He stared at the stones, the sheep now grazing on the other side of the road, and finally at George Fox and Tommy.

"You've ruined my father's herb garden." The boy's imperious tone allowed for no rebuttal. He might have been a judge passing sentence on a prisoner.

A surge of rage rose in Tommy. "Why, we're saving your father's garden. Are you blind?" He clenched his fists and stepped toward the coach.

The boy was about his own age, Tommy noted. His scrawny neck looked as if it could not support his large head. Thin, silky dark hair accented the pallor of his cheekbones. He looked like a living skeleton. Now the boy's face whitened with anger, but he did not reply. His withering glance skimmed off Tommy. Tommy had the curious sensation of being invisible.

The boy in the coach spoke to Old John.

"Bring that man here."

Old John flicked his whip. "You, there. Come over here to Master Dirk."

George Fox obeyed with an easy, graceful movement.

"Who are you?"

Tommy wished Dirk wouldn't talk in such contemptuous tones.

"George Fox."

The big man's complete ease and quietness soothed Tommy as nothing else could have done. He felt a security in Fox's presence, as if nothing bad could ever happen. No, not quite that—more as if there would be guidance no matter what unpleasant incidents came up.

"You're the man my mother talked about." Dirk brooded for a moment, then snapped. "Don't you have any manners? It's only polite to take off your hat in the presence of your superiors."

The words were almost the same as Dirk's father, Squire Grantham, had said only a few hours ago.

"I never take off my hat to anyone."

Dirk sputtered and shrank back a little, as if he could not believe his ears. Why, Tommy thought, no one's ever crossed him before.

"Why, why—" Dirk craned his thin neck. "How dare you speak that way to me? My father could have you thrown in prison."

Fox stood silent.

"Well, why don't you say something? Why are you

staring so? Your—eyes—they're so strange—" Dirk shrank back. For the first time Tommy felt sympathy for the other boy. He, too, had looked into George Fox's eyes and he knew their power.

Fox gazed at Dirk. "I see God's Spirit at work in thee."

"Wha—what are you saying?" Dirk stammered in confusion. "What does he mean?" Dirk appealed to Tommy.

Tommy shook his head. He didn't quite know what Fox meant, but he did know that if George Fox saw God's Spirit working in Dirk, it must be true.

"I see thee helping those who bring God's message to seekers," Fox told Dirk.

"But I couldn't possibly help anybody. I'm ill." Dirk's lips trembled. "The doctor says I can never get well."

His hopeless tone brought a lump of sympathy in Tommy's throat. What would it mean never to run out in the sunshine, and if he did go outside, to be shut up in a carriage all the time?

George Fox was speaking. His rich voice rippled outdoors as it had in the vast reception room. Why, Tommy thought in amazement, his voice could fill the whole world.

A surge of joyous power lifted Fox's voice. "God will heal thee if thou wilt accept His light within thee," he told Dirk.

"You're out of your mind. I haven't walked for five years." All Dirk's cocksureness had gone. "I almost know what you mean." His voice broke. He frowned and grimaced. A gleam came into his eyes. Tommy saw curiosity overcome the other boy. Something else was there, too. Was Dirk beginning to believe?

"Why don't you take off your hat?" For the first time Dirk sounded natural, and Tommy glimpsed a truth. Dirk was really a boy like himself and not just the rich, overbearing, spoiled son of a squire.

"God does not tell men to honor each other by taking off their hats to one another," Fox explained. "All men are equal in the sight of Him."

Dirk frowned a little, then nodded. "Are sick people equal in His sight, too?"

He did not sound like the same boy. Tommy watched him, amazed at his new humility. Or had Dirk been seeking something all along?

"Thou dost not need to be sick in spirit. The Lord's power is over all." Fox's earnestness seemed to impress Dirk. He listened with wide eyes and an expression of yearning.

Tommy himself felt the strange tingling he had felt before in Fox's presence. Dirk was silent, and Fox turned away, taking out his Bible to read as he walked. Tommy saw Dirk struggle with the latch of the coach door.

"Wait, wait. I'm going to walk with you."

At these words, Old John, sitting ramrod stiff on the high coach seat, turned around, a horrified expression on his wrinkled face. "Master Dirk, what are you thinking of? You can't walk. You haven't walked in five years."

"I'm going to walk now. My legs feel strong. Open the door, John."

Old John clambered down and caught hold of the gold handle on the coach door. "Your father won't like it, and you know what happens when he gets angry."

"Open the door, please."

"But Master Dirk, wait. Let me go to the house and get your crutches."

Dirk gestured for Old John to turn the handle. "Help me down."

Old John tottered under Dirk's slight weight. Tommy jumped to help. Dirk was so thin his elbow bones hurt Tommy's hands.

As soon as his feet touched ground, Dirk laughed. The former haughty expression had gone. He looked lighthearted and radiant. "I'm healed! The Lord's power *is* over all, just the way George Fox said. See? I can walk." He tottered a little, then moved slowly but steadily down the road toward the manor house.

Wanting to help Dirk, Tommy imitated every step and screwed up his face, as if that would boost the other boy along.

Every few feet Old John pleaded, "Master Dirk! That's enough for the first time. You'll be laid up in bed."

Dirk took in deep gulps of the warm summer air. "No," he gasped, "I'm healed. I feel it. I'm—" He hesitated. "I'm going to surprise Father, and when George Fox comes back, I'll show him too."

Tommy could see Fox, by this time far down the road in the other direction, still reading his Bible.

"Come with me," Dirk said to Tommy.

"I have to get the sheep in," Tommy replied.

"Then meet me at the kitchen passageway as soon as you are through."

Tommy herded the sheep into the fold without trouble and ran to meet Dirk, just as Celia ran into the yard from the house.

"Oh, Master Dirk! Where were you? Your mother was worried about your staying out so long. I'm supposed to help you."

For a moment the old haughty expression appeared on Dirk's face. "Who are you?"

"I'm Celia. Your mother hired me to help, and this is my brother Tommy. Your father hired him." Celia came forward, hand outstretched. "I thought you couldn't walk. I understood your mother to say—"

"Leave me alone." Dirk pushed her away. His rudeness seemed to hang in the air, and he flushed. "I mean—can't you see I'm walking? It's the first time in five years. Run on ahead and tell Mother."

Celia ran into the house.

Tommy and Dirk walked through the kitchen passageway toward the entrance hall. A girl's voice rose in anger. A man's heavy rumble answered.

"That's my sister," Tommy said, upset. "Was the squire angry about something?"

"Oh, no," Dirk laughed. "It must be the milkmaid or the kitchen maid. Maybe the cream's gone sour or the bread didn't rise."

But in the gloom at the turn of the corridor, Tommy recognized Celia by the flash of her red petticoat and her yellow stockings.

"Celia! What's the matter?"

Celia was leaning backward over the heavy carved chest that almost filled the narrow hall. Nick Hogan was trying to hang a gold chain around her neck.

"Here, take this," he urged. "God rewards His followers with a golden crown."

"No, no! I don't want it," Celia half sobbed.

"Leave my sister alone," Tommy shouted and leaped on Nick Hogan's back. Nick flung him off and whirled around. A spasm of hatred distorted his face. With a violent shove he threw Tommy backward to the floor and dashed toward the front door.

Dirk came toward Tommy and Celia as fast as he could. "What happened?"

"I don't really know," Celia said. "I was coming past this chest and Nick was stooping over it. He saw me and tried to force me to take a locket and chain." She rubbed her arm. "That Nick Hogan is a bad man, yet he talks about God all the time." She sank onto the carved chest and burst into tears.

"Come away from that chest, Celia," Dirk urged. "If Padgett sees anyone near it, he gets terribly upset. He's the steward, and he keeps all the rent money and the family jewels in this chest. He's the only one with a key, besides Father, and he worries about it all the time."

Remembering Nick's strange actions, Tommy examined the padlock. "But, Dirk, look. It's unlocked."

Dirk examined the lock for himself. His face whitened. "I've got to tell Father right away." He braced himself against the wall in his hurry to walk faster. "Come with me." By the time he reached the reception room, he was panting. "Wait just a minute until I catch my breath."

Tommy heard the squire's familiar voice. "I don't understand why your George Fox left the meeting and went off by himself like that, leaving all his so-called Friends to go home by themselves. You say he waits to be moved by the Lord. I don't understand it at all, but at any rate, my gout is much better, not that I think either he or the Lord had anything to do with it."

Dirk pushed the door open and walked in. Tommy and Celia followed. The squire turned with a glare. His mouth dropped open in surprise.

"What's this? What's this?" Squire Grantham heaved himself out of his chair. His stick clattered to the floor. "Where are your crutches?"

Dirk grinned. "I don't need them anymore, Father. I can walk now. It's the Lord's power over all, just the way George Fox said."

The squire, in his astonishment and strong emotion, stepped out on his swollen, bandaged foot, yet only joy showed on his face. Dirk's mother pressed her hands to her heart. Tears streamed down her cheeks.

"The miracle—it's the miracle I've always prayed for. Oh, glory be to God and to His blessed instrument, George Fox. I feel God's glory in this room like a light."

A thunderous pounding sounded at the double doors. The squire, still staring at Dirk, sat down. The pounding continued. Squire Grantham frowned and half turned. Padgett, the steward, burst in, his face ashen. "The great trunk! Master, it's been opened! The first time in twenty years without my knowledge."

"Is the money gone?"

"No, sir, but—"

"Is my wife's jewelry there?"

Padgett's eyes rolled. "I didn't look for it. I don't know."

62

Tommy caught Celia's glance and understood her unspoken words. Nick Hogan must have taken the locket and chain from the chest.

"Stop sniveling, Padgett," the squire said. "Where's the key?"

"Gone—gone—gone." Padgett wrung his hands.

"Call the servants."

Padgett ran out shouting at the top of his voice. From all sides servants scurried to the reception room—the cook from the kitchen, the upstairs maids, the footmen, and in a few moments, the milkmaids, blacksmith, and carpenter. Alarm showed on every face.

The squire scanned the line of servants. "Hmmm. You've all been here a long time—all that is, except those two." He pointed to Celia and Tommy.

"What's your name, girl?"

"Celia Stafford."

The squire's face turned purple. "You're not Parson Stafford's daughter, are you?"

Celia trembled and looked at the floor. "Yes."

"So this is how he gets his revenge? He not only leaves my church, but he tries to rob me."

Tommy stepped forward. "Please, sir, she's my sister. She didn't take anything."

"Your sister? You're a Stafford, too?"

"Yes, sir."

"Aren't you the new shepherd boy?"

"Yes, sir."

Dirk came up beside Tommy. The servants gasped and exclaimed. Tommy knew that Dirk's walking without crutches amazed them. But even this reminder of the miracle healing did not check the squire's anger.

"Keep out of this, my boy," the squire told Dirk. "The children of heretics are not welcome in my house. You're fired. Both of you. Get out. I never want to see you again."

Threat from the Law

In the front hall, Celia burst into tears. Tommy tried to comfort her.

"Don't cry, Celia. Remember, I've been fired, too."

"But you weren't accused of *stealing*." Celia choked out the word. "That's worse than being a heretic. What will Mother say? And that horrid Mrs. Buxby?"

"Nobody will have to know except Mother," Tommy said. "Come on. We'd better start back to the inn."

Celia wiped her eyes on her red petticoat. "When Father comes back, I hope he takes us all to Devon to live." She brightened. "Maybe he's already at the inn."

"But he's only been gone six days, Celia. It's a long trip. It'll take him at least another week to get home."

"By that time everybody in Ulverston will have heard the story about the locket." Celia flipped her skirt defiantly. "Well, let them talk." She sounded more like herself now.

Mrs. Grantham hurried out of the reception room.

When she saw Tommy and Celia, she sighed with relief. "There you are," she said. "I was afraid you had already gone. You must stay here overnight."

Tommy shook his head. "I think we'd better leave, Mrs. Grantham."

The squire's wife put her arms around Celia. "Now, don't you worry about that locket. I know you didn't take it, but the squire gets very upset about things like that. He won't listen to reason. But you can't go home now. There are highwaymen everywhere at night. No one's safe on the roads."

At first, out of pride, Tommy determined not to accept Mrs. Grantham's invitation, but a moment's thought convinced him it would be foolhardy to be on the road at night with highwaymen a menace at every crossroad. He and Celia accepted Mrs. Grantham's offer.

The next morning, she arranged for the coach to take them to the inn. Dirk came, too. When the coach drew up near the kitchen entrance of the manor house, Celia exclaimed with delight. Old John opened the door for her. She stepped inside and perched on the edge of the seat, an expression of bliss on her face. For his part, Tommy had different impressions. Long before the coach reached the main road, he was sure that he had never been so jolted in all his life. Dirk, however, did not seem to mind the bumpy ride.

On a narrow street in Ulverston the coach slowed down.

"John, what's the matter?" Dirk called.

"I can't go any further, Master Dirk. There's a man blocking the street."

The three crowded near the coach window to see. A barefoot man in a white robe trudged ahead.

"He's putting some feathery stuff on his head," Celia said in amazement.

"Probably ashes," Dirk said.

"But why would he do that?" Tommy craned his neck to see better.

"Repent—repent—the time of judgment is at hand," the white-robed man intoned. His voice rose and fell in a mournful wail. "Woe be to false prophets!" He twirled a long, golden chain and locket above his head.

Tommy grabbed Dirk's arm. "That's Nick Hogan. Celia, isn't that the gold locket he tried to give you?"

"Yes, it is," Celia said with conviction. "I remember the extra long chain on it."

Dirk had his hand on the door handle. "That's Mother's locket! I'm sure of it." He bounced in excitement. "I'll tell Father. When he finds out that Nick took the locket and not you, Celia, he'll make it up in some way."

Celia did not answer. Instead, she drew back from the window of the coach. "Look at those two men walking up to Nick." Her voice quivered, and Tommy felt her tremble.

The two men talked to Nick. One man was tall and one was short, with a plaid cloth bound around his head.

"Tommy, it's those highwaymen." Celia's words ended in a shriek.

Tommy gave her a warning nudge. "Sssssh! They'll hear you." He watched the two men. "They're after that gold locket. They're pretending to agree with Nick. Oh, I wish a constable would come along."

"We couldn't prove anything," Dirk said in a shaky, excited voice. "Wait until I tell Father. He'll have them all put in prison." He ordered Old John to force the coach ahead. Tommy and Celia ducked out of sight when the coach lumbered past the two highwaymen and Nick.

At the inn, Old John turned the horses around for the return trip. Dirk leaned out and called, "I'll come back by dogcart as soon as I find out what Father's going to do."

The coach rattled away, but another disturbance took its place—the shrieks and screams of someone in the inn.

Tommy and Celia ran inside. Mother was trying to calm Mrs. Buxby.

"But, Mrs. Stafford," Mrs. Buxby said between wails, "I *can't* forget it. I thought they were gentlemen, and all the time they were highwaymen. To think they would come back and rob a poor widow! What am I going to do?"

"Now, now," Mother soothed, "we settled all this yesterday. Your inn is filled with paying guests—the Friends. They'll soon pay you enough for their lodging to make up what you lost. Ten pounds isn't really very much. Now, do try to recall our discussion. George Fox is coming here today for a meeting, remember?"

Mother cast a puzzled, questioning glance toward Tommy and Celia, as if asking what they were doing at the inn, but Tommy could see this was no time for explanations. Mother had her hands full coping with Mrs. Buxby's continued hysterics. The landlady alternately laughed and screamed, pulling at her hair until it came loose about her ears. Dr. Huber drove up in his carriage. This time Nick Hogan was not in attendance. The doctor strode into the house, stopped when he saw the landlady, and ordered her to be bound.

"So she won't hurt herself," he explained curtly.

"What happened?"

"Two highwaymen came here yesterday when she was alone and robbed her of ten pounds," Mother said.

The doctor nodded. "We'll take a little blood. That'll quiet her." He called for a bowl from the kitchen and rolled up Mrs. Buxby's sleeve.

Tommy looked on fascinated. The doctor pierced the skin at the bend of her elbow and prepared to let the blood drip into the bowl. No blood came. With an amazed look, the doctor probed deeper. Only the slightest red showed. With an exclamation of disgust, Dr. Huber pulled down Mrs. Buxby's sleeve. The landlady wailed and moaned in a rhythm that reminded Tommy of Nick Hogan ranting on the streets.

There was a knock at the door. Tommy ran to open it. George Fox stood outside, his big body filling the doorway as it had once before. At the sight of him, Mrs. Buxby began to shriek.

The doctor bowed. "Well, my friend, Mr. Fox. You have come most propitiously. Perhaps you can heal this woman as you have healed others."

The doctor accepted his fee from one of the Friends standing silently by, and bowed. His sword flipped up in back as he did so. He left the inn without another word, appearing to ignore Mrs. Buxby's redoubled cries.

"Unbind her," George Fox said.

"But she is violent. She may hurt herself," one of the Friends objected.

"Unbind her, and let her alone."

When Mrs. Buxby was freed, she shuddered and rubbed her arms. Her head shook spasmodically. She opened her mouth to scream again.

"Peace," George Fox commanded. "Be still in the name of the Lord."

A marvelous stillness came over Mrs. Buxby. Her contorted features smoothed out. A glow of happiness lit her face.

"Thanks be to God," she whispered. "What has been happening? Oh, yes, the Friends are here. And you're George Fox. I ask your pardon for all the things I've said against you. May I be a Friend, too?"

Murmurs of rejoicing rose on all sides.

During the meeting of Friends, Tommy made a discovery. Friends took off their hats during prayer or when they were inspired to speak because they honored God. The entire inn parlor was filled with people. Some sat on the stairway, some on benches and stools. For a long time no one moved or spoke. The peacefulness grew and expanded. Tommy waited for the inward quickening which he had experienced before. This time he was not surprised when it came.

After a silence, George Fox burst out in his deep, resonant voice, "Friends, the Holy Scriptures were given forth by the Spirit of God, and all people must first come to the Spirit of God in themselves, by which they might know God and Christ. In this Spirit, ye may have fellowship with the Son and with the Father and with the Scriptures and with one another. Without this Spirit, ye can know neither God nor Christ nor the Scriptures."

Fox's words filled Tommy with a longing to experience the Spirit for himself. If only Father would come back soon, he would feel the same desire—that is, if he would only listen to George Fox.

After the meeting, the Friends accompanied Fox into town, where he would speak to the people as the Spirit moved him. The Staffords stayed with Mrs. Buxby, and Tommy and Celia at last could tell the story of the stolen locket and chain.

The sound of horses' hooves startled them. Dirk and Old John were outside in a two-wheeled cart drawn by one horse. Dirk started talking so fast Tommy could hardly understand him.

"Father's going to have Nick Hogan arrested and the highwaymen, too. I have to go right back. The swelling in Father's foot is all gone and we're going to Ireland to visit family friends—the Penns. There's a boy my age. His name is William.° He's never seen me without crutches. Wait until I tell him about George Fox and all the other exciting things. I'll see you when I get back."

After Dirk left, Tommy felt a curious letdown. He sat in the parlor with the others. When a loud knock sounded at the door, Tommy sighed, disliking to move. He looked at Mother, sitting with her hands folded. Mrs. Buxby nodded in a chair. Celia tapped her toe on the floor. The knock sounded again, imperious this time.

"Open the door in the name of our protector, Oliver Cromwell," a heavy male voice called. At the

---

°William Penn, the founder of Pennsylvania, was born October 14, 1644.

71

same time the latch clicked and a tall man with lined, weather-beaten features came in. His stern, resolute air brought a chill into the room. There was something ominous in the way he stood looking around.

"I'm Constable Jarvis."

Mrs. Buxby jerked awake and blinked, but said nothing.

"Which of you is Celia Stafford?" Constable Jarvis asked.

Mother stared at the constable and moved close to Celia.

"I am," Celia said.

"I hereby place you under arrest."

In the sudden hush, Tommy could almost hear the blood rush to his head. His body throbbed in a nightmare sensation of unreality. Mother gasped, controlled herself, and put her arm around Celia.

"Arrest?" Mother asked. "For what?"

"Squire Grantham has a warrant here for Celia Stafford's arrest. He claims she took a valuable gold locket and chain from his house."

"But didn't his son tell him? Nick Hogan took the necklace. All three of us saw him with it," Celia said.

Tommy had never admired his sister Celia as much as at that moment. She sounded composed and neither scared nor sassy.

Celia started to explain further. "He was—"

"Save your explanations for the court, miss," Constable Jarvis said. "I am here only to do my duty." He nodded to two men waiting behind him. "Take this girl to Ulverston prison."

"Prison?" Mother's lips trembled. "Take me instead.

72

She's only a girl. She can't be thrown in a place with rogues and thieves—"

"Save your breath, madam," Constable Jarvis ordered. "This isn't easy for any of us, but it is the law. You do respect the law, don't you? Aren't you a Quaker?"

Mother nodded. Her eyes filled with tears. She dropped her arms to her side. "May the Lord's will be done," she said in a half-sob.

Constable Jarvis and his men took Celia outside and helped her onto a horse. Tommy clenched his fists, knowing there was nothing anyone could do. If only Father were here—he could surely do something. But Father was in Devon. Then the solution came to Tommy.

"Mother, I'll go find George Fox. He'll help. I know he will."

Mother nodded in a dazed way. "Yes, he is our only hope. Try to find him."

With a heart heavy with dread, yet swelling with new born hope, Tommy hurried to the market square. It did not take long to find the crowd of people and the familiar white hat showing above their heads. The people surrounding Fox were so close-knit that Tommy could not push his way through. It took him a few minutes to realize that this was not a crowd of interested people and Friends, but a coldly hostile mob. Nevertheless, there was not much action or movement. At least no one was wielding sticks.

Tommy wriggled through at last. George Fox stood silent as he often did, but since he did not seem to be in meditation, Tommy ran up to his side.

"George Fox, it's my sister Celia. They've arrested

her and brought her here to the Ulverston prison. Can you help me get her out?"

A guffaw split the air. Tommy turned in astonishment. Constable Jarvis stood near George Fox. His assistant, one of the men who took Celia away, doubled over in merriment.

"Let the halt help the lame," the assistant said, wiping tears off his cheeks. "Young man, you've certainly come to the right place for help."

Tommy stood bewildered. His words sounded all right, but his tone of voice did not.

"Sure, he'll be glad to help Celia. In fact, he's going over there right now, soon as the papers come." He slapped his knee. "Second one of these ranters we've run in today."

Tommy could make no sense out of the assistant's remarks. He turned to George Fox. "We knew you would help us. It'd be just a little miracle for you, but a big miracle for us. We've never had anybody in prison before, and besides, Celia didn't take the locket."

A man made his way through the onlookers and handed folded papers to Constable Jarvis. The constable's assistant put his hand on Tommy's shoulder. "Yes, my boy," he said in mock concern, "it must be a pretty hard blow, all right, but here's a harder. You see those papers?"

Tommy shrank back from the assistant with intense dislike. "Yes."

"Any help Mr. Fox will be giving people from now on will be from his headquarters—the prison house. Those papers, my boy, are the warrant for his arrest."

Tommy turned away in despair.

74

7

Shadow of Death

A crowd of people, some hooting and jeering, some with heads down and hands folded in prayer, followed George Fox through the streets of Ulverston to the hall of justice. A woman ran up to Fox and clawed at his face with her fingernails. A constable pushed her aside. The woman spit in contempt.

"Let me at him," she cried. "I'll pluck the very hair from his head."

George Fox gazed at her, and the woman shrieked. "Look at his eyes!" She backed away. "Do not pierce me with your looks. Keep your eyes off me."

Fox's steady gaze did not waver. "I direct you to Christ Jesus, your inward teacher. Build on Him, the rock and foundation that does not change. His Spirit dwells within you."

Howls of rage from the crowd met his remarks. "Blasphemer! Heretic!" they called.

Tommy sensed a terrifying, unleashed violence behind the hoarse voices. The Friends in the group kept silent and pressed with steadfastness down the street, yielding neither to pressure nor to taunts.

At the door of the hall of justice a girl ran out. She saw the crowd, gasped, and pressed against the wall of the building. Tommy recognized his sister Celia, and a new terror filled his mind. Had she tried to escape? Could she be that foolish? He forced his way to her through the crowd.

"Celia! What are you doing here? How did you get away?"

She looked up with a glad cry. "Oh, Tommy! I'm free. It was all a mix-up. The squire had put out the warrant for my arrest before Dirk got there and told him about Nick. Then he sent out a warrant to arrest Nick Hogan instead." She hugged Tommy. "It's so good to be free. But what are all these people doing here?"

"George Fox has been arrested," Tommy began, but he was interrupted by shouts of joy.

"Judge Fell won't serve the warrant!" the word went around. "George Fox is free!"

As soon as they realized Fox was truly free, Tommy and Celia hurried to the inn to tell Mother the news. To their joyous surprise, Father was there. He grabbed Celia and swung her off her feet in a hug. Everyone laughed and talked at the same time, but somehow the whole story came out.

"We are going to Devon as soon as we can get ready," Father announced. "Your uncle paid up all my inheritance to date, but even so, I think it will be better to live among people who know our family."

"But we can't go, Father," Celia cried out. "We're Friends now."

"Friends?" Father stiffened in anger.

"Yes. George Fox is our leader. Father, you must see him. Now!" Celia pleaded.

At first Father refused to listen to anything about the Friends. Then the landlady, now going by her full Quaker name, Agnes Buxby, appealed to him to help her with the work of the inn. Father agreed, especially when he learned George Fox was to travel through the country preaching. Months later the Friends in Ulverston learned that George Fox had been imprisoned in Carlisle. Mother determined to go with Tommy and Celia to visit him.

Father gave in. "You can't go alone," he said shortly. "Too many highwaymen." He arranged for the family to take the trip by horseback.

At Carlisle, Father refused to go to George Fox's trial. "I'll wait for you until it's over," he promised in a resigned voice.

While Mother remained behind to try to persuade Father to see the trial, Tommy and Celia found themselves borne along by a crowd of people into the hall where the trial was being held. In a few moments a side door opened. A guard brought out a man dressed in white robes.

Celia gasped. Tommy recognized Nick Hogan. What was he doing in Carlisle? He must have thought he had a message like George Fox and traveled around preaching his false notions.

Another guard brought in George Fox. Both prisoners were brought to stand before the judge, dignified in his red robes. The judge stared first at Nick Hogan's white garb, now dirty and torn, and then at George Fox's bulky form.

"What be these you have brought here in court?" the judge asked the constable.

"Prisoners, my lord."

"Tell the prisoner on my left to take off his hat," the judge instructed, with a nod to Fox.

Fox appeared not to hear the constable's instructions.

"Take off your hat, I say," the judge said directly to him.

Fox still made no reply and he did not move.

"Do you know where you are?" The judge's tone threatened punishment. "Don't you know enough to show honor where honor is due? The court commands you to take off your hat. Perhaps you need a smart stroke of the whip to persuade you."

In quiet dignity, Fox replied, "Men are not made to honor each other, to rank one another because of material things. It may be that my hat offends thee, but hast thou brought me here only because of my hat?"

The judge ignored the question. "Why do you say *thou* and *thee*?" he asked in a cutting tone. "You are but a fool and idiot for speaking so. 'Tis our custom to say *you* to social superiors and *thou* to inferiors."

Fox answered by asking a question himself. "Are they who translated the Scriptures fools and idiots? They made the grammar in this way—*thou* to one and *you* to more than one. Art thou arresting me because I follow the Scriptures. If so, why not imprison the Bible?"

A roar of laughter swept through the courtroom. People repeated the remark to one another, nodding and laughing.

78

The judge's face grew as red as his robes. "Another outburst like this and I will clear the court." He waited until the last whisper died away.

Tommy watched Fox with admiration. The big man seemed both at ease and resolute in his hour of trial. Nick Hogan, on the other hand, shifted his feet, scratched his head, or twitched his shoulders.

"Why am I arrested?" Fox asked.

The judge motioned for the papers to be brought. "You have the effrontery to pose as a minister, yet you have no education."

"Being educated at Oxford or Cambridge is not enough to qualify men as ministers of Christ," Fox replied. "The Lord did not choose any of the wise and learned to be the first messengers of His blessed truth to men. Consult thy Bible. Now, what is it I have done? Read the charge."

"Are you in authority in this court, or am I?" the judge replied in angry tones. "Your charge shall not be read." He flung the papers down. They scattered and the clerk picked them up.

"It ought to be," Fox said in ringing tones. "It concerns my life and liberty. If I have done anything worthy of prison or death, let all the country know it."

The spectators began to murmur. The judge snatched the papers from the clerk.

"Herewithal is George Fox," he read in loud tones, "of Drayton-in-the-Clay, in Leicestershire, which he pretends to be the place of his habitation. He goes under the name of Quaker and acknowledges himself to be such. He has spread several papers tending to the disturbance of the public peace and cannot render any lawful cause of coming into these parts."

A strange fear crept into Tommy. Why didn't the law recognize God's work? Why did God Himself make it so hard for people to serve Him? Yet one look at Fox convinced Tommy that the big, quiet man was perfectly content to accept whatever hardship came his way.

The judge continued. "He refuses to give surety of his good behavior. Therefore, in the name of the Lord Protector, may he be received and safely kept in prison." The judge's mouth twisted in a scornful smile. "I shall uphold the law."

"But that is not the law. There is nothing definite in such a charge," Fox began, but Nick Hogan interrupted. Turning partly to Fox and partly to the spectators, Nick extended his arm toward Fox.

"This man says he is Christ." Nick's accusation rolled through the room like thunder.

After a second of stunned silence, an ominous growl spread over the room. Tommy sensed that people believed Nick Hogan. He was amazed. Couldn't they see Nick Hogan was out of his head?

The judge leaned forward as if ready to pounce. "Do you say you are Christ?"

"No" Fox said. "I am nothing. Christ is all." The love, humility, and assurance in his voice quieted everyone. Tommy felt relief. How could the judge fail to feel God's Spirit in Fox?

Nick Hogan must have sensed the turn of feeling. "May it please you, my lord," he told the judge in silky tones, "this man took me aside and told me how serviceable I might be for his design. He said he could raise 40,000 men at an hour's warning and in-

80

volve the nation into blood and bring in the king."[*]
Nick looked around, as if waiting for an uproar. It
began immediately.

This time there were openly voiced threats, hisses,
and catcalls. Tommy felt as if he were in a boat on
high seas at the mercy of the waves. Voices around
him rose and fell in tones of contempt and loathing.

"How do you answer the charge of treason, Mr.
Fox?" he asked after the crowd became silent.

Fox turned on Nick. Fox looked more terrible in his
mild firmness than if he had threatened Nick with
gestures or angry words. "God will confound thy lies
and wickedness and envy," Fox said. "He will set
His truth over all." Fox began to tremble. A hush
fell over the courtroom. "Thou art a Judas," he told
Nick, "and thy end shall be as Judas'. This is the
word of Christ through me to thee."

Murmurs of awe and shocked belief ran through
the room. "A prophecy—it's a prophecy."

"Order in the court!" the judge roared, but the
spectators would not be silenced.

"They say he foresees Oliver Cromwell's death!"
someone said.

"He says there will be a big fire in London, de-
stroying almost the whole city."[**]

"He foresaw disgrace to a high official."

The remarks passed from one to another. The
judge raised his arm as if to strike Fox. The wide
red sleeves of his robe dipped and opened like the
wings of a monstrous bird.

---

[*]For many years such plots had stirred England. A charge of treason was bound to
touch off violent reactions.

[**]Fox had a vision of the Great Fire of 1666 when almost all of London was destroyed
a long time before it happened.

"I declare a fifteen-minute recess. See that order is brought to this court," the judge commanded the constable and his men, then turned and fled out a side door, his robe flapping behind him.

The law officers tried to clear the courtroom, but no one would leave. The prisoners' guards mingled with the crowd, trying to bring order. Tommy saw his chance. He was burning with a question he wanted to ask Fox. Pulling Celia behind him, Tommy squirmed through the milling crowd to Fox's side.

"George Fox, there is something I must know," Tommy said. "Is it God's will that you—" Tommy corrected himself and used the plain language of the Quakers, "that thou goest to prison?"

To Tommy's utter astonishment, Fox chuckled. "I once asked God why He made it so hard for me to serve Him. He let me know that it was needful for me to have a sense of all conditions in the world. How can I speak to all conditions without experiencing all conditions? Then I realized the infinite love of God."

"*Love?*" It was the last word Tommy had expected to hear. He could have understood that going to prison might be God's punishment, but how could it be a mark of God's love?

"Yes," Fox said. "God fills my heart with infinite desire to serve Him—and He also provides the way. Canst thou understand this?"

Tommy thought a moment. His ideas about God were being turned topsy-turvy. "Is going to prison a way to serve God?"

"Yes. I am set here for a service which He has for me to do," Fox said.

"But the way people are acting, what if something awful happened?" Tommy did not dare express his fear.

"Fear not. I shall be delivered when I have completed my service for God at this place."

Tommy began to understand something. "My father left the Church of England. He was a parson back in Ulverston. Did God tell him to leave the church so as to serve Him better?"

"It could well be. There has been a quickening of spirit all over England in the last few years."

Then a terrible thought came to Tommy. "But will my father be put in prison, too, among thieves and murderers?"

"There are many good people in prison, put there unjustly," George Fox said. "It is not the material prisons that are so harsh, though they are bad enough, but the inner prison of our selfish selves, in which no light shines, to which these people have no key."

"But who has a key to that kind of prison?" Tommy asked.

"Christ is the key. He opens the door of light, life, and love."

Before Tommy could ask more, a guard with bristly red hair pushed him aside. "Children don't belong here. Run on home."

Tommy was determined not to leave until he saw what happened to George Fox. When the judge came out, Tommy and Celia watched from the back of the courtroom. The judge singled out the red-haired guard and waited for the people to quiet down.

"Muggs," the judge announced in steely tones, "put

this man in prison until the next session. Do not let any living flesh come near him. He is not fit to be talked to by men. And, Muggs," the judge added in still harsher tones, "the people must be kept down at all costs. If there is any uprising, you may have to take sterner measures. You understand me?"

Muggs nodded. He and two other guards led Fox toward a side door. Fox turned to the spectators.

"Friends, I'm being imprisoned for the sake of Christ, the great Prophet who speaks from heaven," he called.

"You have good lungs," someone shouted.

"If my voice were five times louder, I should lift it up and sound it out for Christ's sake, for whose cause I stand this day before the judgment seat of the law, but there is a higher seat before which you must all be brought to give an account. Prepare yourselves! God's Spirit dwells within each of you. . . ."

A violent outcry from some of the spectators met Fox's words. People stood up and waved their arms. Quite a few stormed out of the courtroom. Others, to make room, stood up. Once on their feet, they were pushed toward the doors. Tommy and Celia were swept along with the jostling crowd to the outside courtyard. The walls of the prison yard loomed menacingly. The limbs of a huge tree overhung the street. To Tommy, the outstretched branches seemed to beckon a grim invitation.

The group of aroused spectators streamed toward a wide gate at the corner of the prison yard. Tommy steered Celia to a smaller gate farther down. They could see both the crowd and the prison yard from where they stood. Two burly guards thrust Fox through the heavy wooden door of the prison house. One of the guards took up guard duty by the door. The other strolled into the yard. As he passed by the small gate, Tommy called out to him, "May we visit George Fox?"

The guard whirled. "George Fox! That man's dangerous. Why would nice children like you want to see a man like George Fox?"

"We are Friends," Tommy explained.

The guard peered through the grating. "Don't you know that all over England they're putting Friends in prison as fast as they can catch them? Be on your way before you're thrown in prison, too."

The guard hurried off to join his companions. Muggs, the red-haired guard, conferred with his men, pointing to the Friends clustered near the gate and to the unruly mob back of them.

"Would you like to see your Mr. Fox?" Muggs called out to the Friends. A roar of assent met his words, not from the Friends, who had answered simply, but from the restless people pressing near.

Muggs gestured toward the prison house. Two men went inside and brought Fox out. Outside the walls, the shouts and whistles increased. Some of the people began to ram the entrance gate.

Tommy felt a cold, frightening sensation down his spine. He watched Muggs gesture toward the large limb overhanging the wall, take a rope from a fellow guard's hands, and fashion a noose. With a swift movement, Muggs slipped the noose over Fox's head.

"You're sure you want to see Mr. Fox?" Muggs shouted.

"Yes, yes." The answer came from the Friends.

With expectant looks they watched the gate.

The horrible meaning of what was about to happen penetrated Tommy's mind. Rising terror choked him. Celia hid her face on Tommy's shoulder. He knew she understood, too.

"Any last words, Mr. Fox?" Muggs sang out.

Resolutely Fox answered, "I am ready. I never feared death, nor sufferings. I am an innocent, peaceable man, free from stirrings and plottings, and one that seeks the good of all men in the Spirit of God."

His calm words and serene face steadied Tommy. Muggs made a swift, chopping movement with his hand. The other men started to pull the rope that would show Fox to the Friends—but show him as a dead man.

Preacher in Jail

As the guards raised George Fox to his tiptoes, Fox's white hat fell off. A guard picked it up and clapped it on Fox's head.

"Careful of his hat, boys," he shouted. "He wants to keep it on."

Tommy shuddered at the cruel joke. The guards laughed and strained at the rope. There was a thunderous crackling. The branch on which the rope was slung split full length and crashed behind George Fox. With cries of amazement and alarm, the guards flung the rope away and scrambled out into the open.

"It's the hand of God."

"George Fox is under divine protection."

"God's curse is on us all."

They looked at each other in consternation, and with one impulse flew off like chaff in the wind, looking over their shoulders. Fox stood until one of the guards with hesitant steps came back to unbind him. With an uneasy look toward the sky, as if expecting a thunderbolt, the guard motioned to Fox to go into the prison house. Tommy glimpsed Fox's face, calm and resolute as always. What unshakable faith! Tommy yearned to follow in Fox's footsteps and show the same courage. He vowed to himself that he too would somehow, someway, dedicate himself to God's service. Full of his new resolve, he found Father at the inn and poured out his feelings to him.

"Perhaps I should see this man," Father said. "Are you sure he isn't a ranter of some kind? Isn't he out of his head?"

"Oh, no, Father." Tommy described the miracle of Fox's injured hand. "I saw it with my own eyes, and so did Mother and Celia. And, Father, he says churches are nothing but stones and wood. The real church is inside of us, because that's where God's Spirit is."

Father appeared dazed. "For the first time, things are beginning to make sense. That's the idea I've been reaching for myself—and I didn't recognize it. I know I must see Mr. Fox now. Perhaps he can help me see what I am to do in the future."

The jailer, a swarthy man with downturned mouth, met the Staffords at the door. He reached for the money Father offered and seemed never to have heard about the judge's orders to keep people away from Fox.

"Who's that out there?" a woman's sharp voice rose out of the gloomy hallway.

"Visitors," the jailer replied. In a whisper he said, "That's my wife. She's crippled. Sits in a chair there at the end of the hall. She and the dog guard the place." He led the Staffords down cellar steps to a basement room. Horrible odors of stench and decay rose from the damp dirt floor.

"Is this the only place you have?" Father sounded horrified.

"That's all he wanted to pay for," the jailer said. "You can talk to him through this grating." He pointed to a barred door.

Tommy peeked through into a room blackened with the smoke of rushlights. Unspeakable filth covered the floor. Mildewed straw lay in blackened bunches in one corner. Tommy was shocked. Did Fox have to sleep in this room? Was the straw supposed to be a bed?

George Fox sat on a stool in the middle of the room, his arms clasped around his knees. He looked serene and did not seem surprised when Father introduced himself. Tommy saw at once that Father was impressed with Fox's dignity and peaceful air. Even in these vile surroundings, Fox without question was living a spiritual life.

"You can't stay here," Father began. "Won't the Friends put up bail for you?"

"I do not consent that any shall be bound for me," Fox said.

A disturbance sounded throughout the prison house. Someone began to stamp and shout. At once prisoners in other rooms took up the beat, pounding walls and howling. A dog's terrifying growl sounded above the turmoil. Within a minute quiet reigned.

Fox did not appear to notice the dog's howls. "I have learned already that many of these prisoners have been here for months. It is not right to confine people in jail for so long, learning badness of one another. I hope in time the prisons will be reformed. I shall write one of my letters about this and have it printed and sent to the magistrates."°

In the silence, a man's voice chanted, "Doom— doom to Ulverston. Doom to the squire and his gold. I am chosen of God to be His instrument of destruction."

"That's Nick Hogan," Tommy said, startled. He told the story to Father, not mentioning Fox's prophecy. He would tell that later.

"Though all the spirits and devils in hell are here," Fox said, "remember, over them all is the power of God."

When the Staffords left, Father sought out the jailer. "At least, get some dry straw for Mr. Fox to sleep on."

"My wife says no."

"Who is master here, you or your wife?" Father asked.

"She is. She beats me with her quarterstaff if I come within reach."

From down the hall, his wife called out in rage, "Who are these people?"

The jailer led the Staffords to a little room off the hall. A woman sat in the doorway in a large frame chair with red blankets tucked about her. Her face was the color of smoke. Her malicious-looking eyes gleamed black and bitter and her mouth twisted in greedy hope.

"You a friend of that man Fox?" she asked.

"Yes."

°The Quakers began prison reform in England. Through their efforts, prisoners were allowed to do weaving and other hand occupations.

"Can't you afford to rent a better place for him?"

Father looked startled. "Of course." He drew out money.

"Here. Give it to me." The jailer's wife leaned forward and grabbed the money. She counted it over and over and tucked it into a bag tied at her waist.

On their next visit, the Staffords found Fox in the same loathsome place. When Father questioned the jailer, he shook his head.

"Don't make no trouble," he said. "My wife will set the dog on you. Mr. Fox is out in the yard, preaching to the thieves and felons." He led the Staffords down a dark hall to the back.

Prisoners slouched about the yard sullenly watching Fox.

"What makes you think you can help us?" one taunted. "You are in prison yourself. Do you have a key to let yourself out?"

"Christ is the heavenly key," Fox told the man. "He Himself has come to teach you. His grace will teach you how to live, what to do, and what to deny. He is a free teacher to all of you."

"Let God free me from this prison," another called, "and then I'll believe anything you say."

"The physical prison here need not make you prisoners," Fox said. "You have made of yourselves a prison. God did not intend for people to live in the light of the material world but in His eternal Spirit. He is the key to spiritual life, eternal life."

The jailer interrupted. "Time to go in."

"Thou saidst I might come," Fox protested in a mild tone.

"And now I say come back in."

The prisoners protested. "Let him stay—let him stay."

As the uproar increased, the jailer looked frightened. He ran back inside and came out with a quarterstaff and a huge mastiff.

"We'll show you who runs this prison," the jailer said. The dog looked eagerly ahead, his loose jowls dripping saliva, and his teeth showing in a savage snarl.

The prisoners quieted, but Fox, disregarding cries of warning, started toward the dog. Instead of leaping on Fox, the dog sniffed, whined, and lay down at Fox's feet, with its head between its paws.

With a look of stupefaction, the jailer lowered his quarterstaff, stared at the silent prisoners, tugged at the dog, and went back into the prison house.

The jailer's wife screamed in rage. Her words carried out into the yard. "You must be lying! That man Fox is a rogue—a witch. He skipped out of hell when the devil was asleep."

"Wife," the jailer said in a troubled tone, "I had such a vision come over me. I saw the Day of Judgment, and I saw George Fox there! I am afraid. We have done him such wrong."

He came back outside, requesting Fox to go back to his cell. Fox obeyed, and the Staffords followed.

Tommy could see the change in Father. Before he had met Fox, he spoke contemptuously of the "street preacher," but now he asked eager questions about the new doctrine of the Christ Spirit within.

"There is an anointment within man to teach him. The Lord teaches His people Himself," Fox began.

94

The powerful vibrancy of Fox's person seemed to convince Father that the Spirit of God lived in this man. Fox talked of the missionary work by the Friends—how they were going two by two over England, speaking to those who were receptive, obeying all laws, never taking up arms, even to protect themselves, and never taking off their hats to honor men.

Father paced the damp basement room. Tommy sensed his excitement as the two men talked.

"I have studied the Scriptures for many years, and I've been a preacher in the church—"

Fox glanced up. "Not church," he said with his usual gentleness. "The steeple houses are not churches. The true church is within."

"Yes, yes, of course." Father almost babbled in his embarrassment. "I mean, how could I have preached in the steeple houses and followed their rites and rituals? How could I fail to understand that Christ's Spirit directs every man from within—not without?"

Fox smiled. "I too spent many years studying the Scriptures, yet I knew them not until by revelation. He who had the key did open and as the Father of Life drew me to His Son by His Spirit. He it was that opened to me when I was shut up and had neither hope nor faith."

"Mr. Fox," Father said in a voice trembling with earnestness, "I want to be a Friend. I want to join this great crusade of men who bring such light to the people of England."

Again Fox smiled. "I already know and have known since we first met that thou art one of us. Thou wilt indeed be a missionary for the Friends. God has let me know that, but it will not be in England."

"Not in England?" Father appeared baffled. "But where else can the light be brought? I know no other language—except Latin, of course." He smiled a little. "Where do you mean?"

"I mean America," Fox said. "The savages there need the light. There, too, I see a great new world in the future, with many kinds of people. They know it not, but they all will be seeking for the Christ within. Wouldst thou be willing to go to America?"

Without hesitation, Father replied, "Of course."

When the visit ended, Father asked Fox, "Are you getting enough food? Tommy and I will bring your meals to you if you are having any difficulty."

Fox shook his head. "I thank thee, but I have made other arrangements. When thou art to come again to see me, thou wilt be unmistakably impressed to do so." With this, Fox dismissed them.

The word *America* rang in Tommy's ears all the way home. Father said nothing, but Tommy could tell by the look on his face that he was in America already in imagination.

"Elizabeth," he called in exuberance when he entered the inn, "he *recognized* me. He knew my mission for God before I even knew it myself."

"Your mission?" Mother looked hopeful.

"Yes, yes. We'll have to go back to Ulverston at once and start packing. Oh, it was God's will that all our household things should be taken away from us. What marvelous foresight! We won't need them now."

Mother sighed. "We'll just have to buy more furniture in Devon."

"Devon? Who said anything about Devon?"

"Isn't that where we're going to move?" Mother asked with a quizzical glance.

"Oh, no, no, Elizabeth." Father sounded a bit impatient. "We're going to America."

"America?" Mother faltered and groped for a chair, never taking her eyes off Father.

"Why, yes, of course," Father said briskly. "That's where our mission is to be."

"Mission? What mission?"

For the first time, Father seemed to realize that Mother had not been with him that afternoon. He sat down and recounted his discussion with George Fox.

Within a few days the idea of America began to seem quite natural to Tommy. Even red Indians sounded like people seeking for the great light of Christ—in spirit if not by name.

On the tenth day Father took Tommy to see George Fox. As they entered the prison house, he kept saying, "I feel this is the day." They found Fox looking haggard and drawn. At the same time, his face glowed with an almost unearthly serenity.

"Hast thou not eaten since we saw thee last?" Father used the plain language of the Quakers with ease, Tommy noticed.

"Nay," George Fox answered. "I was impressed to fast during this period."

"Ten days without food?" Tommy blurted. Before he could question further, the jailer and his guards brought two men down the hall. The shorter of the two had no ear.

"Father!" Tommy caught hold of Father's coat sleeve. "There go the highwaymen. It's Black Bart and his friend."

The short man kicked and shouted, flinging his arms up trying to break away from the guards.

"Calm down there, Stubby," the guards said. "Jailer, get the dog."

Stubby sneered, but when the dog leaped upon him and pushed him backward with two huge paws, Stubby yelled.

"Take that monster off me. I'll go quietly."

The jailer's wife called out in a high-pitched voice, "Bring those men to me."

The jailer took the men to her. Tommy heard her say in a conniving whine, "I understand you are Black Bart. You know you can have many privileges in prison if you have the money." She lowered her voice, and Tommy could hear no more.

When Father had finished discussing the mission to America with Fox, the Staffords returned to Ulverston to prepare for their journey. Late one night the bellman hallooed outside the inn.

"How odd!" Agnes Buxby said. "The bellman never comes this far. I wonder what the news is."

The bellman began to chant. "Lock your door! Lock your door! Prisoners at large! Black Bart and two accomplices have returned to Ulverston. All able-bodied men come forth to join the search. These felons are armed and dangerous. Prisoners at large!"

Tommy and Celia helped close casements and bolt doors. What if Black Bart came back to the inn with Stubby, his companion? But who was the third accomplice? How could the people in the inn defend themselves against three desperate men?

9

Treacherous Escape

The bellman brought startling news the next day. A large sum of rent money had been stolen from the squire's house, and the three prisoners at large were blamed for it. The two highwaymen, Black Bart and Stubby, were wanted all over that part of the country, but somehow they had always managed to bribe their guards and gain freedom.

"Did you know that Nick Hogan—the doctor's servant, if you remember—is one of them now?" the bellman asked. "Nick knew the inside of Squire Grantham's house like his own hand, being there so much with the doctor tending to the squire's gout. He should never have stolen from the squire, of all people. The squire will never rest until they're all in prison." The bellman shifted his bell to the other hand and spoke in a confidential tone. "Word has got around that George Fox prophesied Nick would end like Judas."

The next day the news bell pealed louder than ever in front of the inn.

"Nick Hogan has hanged himself out in a field near town," the bellman said in an awed voice. "That George Fox *is* a prophet, I do believe."

But George Fox was still in prison at Carlisle. The Staffords postponed their plans to go to America until Fox was freed and joined other Friends for another trip to Carlisle to wait for the next court session.

The Friends learned that many of their number were being imprisoned on any pretext. Magistrates stationed guards on town streets and highways.

One day after Father had gone to the Carlisle prison house to talk to George Fox, Mother insisted on visiting the prison, too, with Tommy and Celia. On the way, they saw two constables on guard at a turn of the road.

"Stop! Where are you going?" one asked.

"To visit a Friend," Mother said. "Has something happened?"

"We are on the lookout for suspicious persons."

"Like highwaymen?" Tommy asked.

"We've had plenty of trouble with them," the constable acknowledged, "but these days we are looking for other people. But come to think of it, these people we're looking for are like highwaymen, aren't they?" He nudged his companion.

"Yes," the other man replied. "They've stolen the hearts of ignorant people. They're thieves, all right." He smirked, appearing pleased with his own words.

"We'd better not go on, then," Mother said.

"Oh," the constable said in a grudging tone, "these people aren't violent, but they're stirring up a lot of mischief in England." He added with scorn, "Friends, they call themselves."

Mother drew herself up. "Why, the Friends are law-abiding, God-fearing people. What laws have they broken?"

"They have meetings, and that's forbidden. How do we know they're not getting up an army? We're putting these Friends in prison as fast as we catch them."

Mother did not hesitate. "Then you'd better start with us. We're Friends, and if you insist on being unjust, you'd better take us to prison right now."

The constable stroked his chin. "Well, Ma'am, your case don't seem to be what we're looking for. They have to do a little something out of the way first. You go on, but I'd advise you to think twice about belonging to a group of radicals like the Friends."

As the Staffords walked on, Tommy could not resist looking back at the constables. How could such sincere-appearing people believe such things? He decided to ask Fox about it.

At the prison house, George Fox answered his question in two words. "Fear and ignorance. People who do not have the light of God within them act blindly. I've been hearing about what is happening to the Friends. Watchmen take them before justices, where they are discharged because there is no real cause for their arrest; then in the next town another watchman arrests them and takes them before other justices. It is not in accordance with the law. I have written a letter to the magistrates and I am going to have it printed."

"May we hear it?" Mother asked.

Fox took out a sheet of paper and began to read: "Ye pretend liberty of conscience, yet shall not one

101

carry a letter to a Friend, nor men visit their friends, nor visit prisoners, nor carry a book about them." Fox looked up indignantly. "These be well-armed men, too," he went on, "against a people that have not so much as a stick in their hands, who are in scorn called Quakers because they confess and witness the true light."

The jailer brought in a man with a notice. "Court clerk," the jailer announced.

The clerk read a summons in a loud, droning voice. "Ordered, that George Fox do appear before the Council at its next session." He pointed to the bottom of the sheet. "And there's my signature."

On the appointed day the courtroom filled up early. The major, sheriff, aldermen, learned recorder, justices, and jury came in. The clerk, with quill pen and paper, took his place. Tommy and Celia sat with Father and Mother in the hot steamy room. Prisoners filed in. Their clothes stank of close confinement in the filthy prison quarters. The chief justice beckoned to the clerk, who brought in a bouquet of herbs. The justice buried his face in it. A bit of the fragrance wafted to Tommy's nostrils. The heat and stench were making him sick to his stomach. Mother held a handkerchief to her nose.

Tommy caught a glimpse of a quiet woman about the same age as Mother. She sat looking as cool and composed as if she were in the drawing room of a great house. Her calm, sweet features showed no sign of disdain or displeasure.

People around Tommy whispered her name. "That's Margaret Fell." The whispers went around the room.

Tommy looked at Margaret Fell as often as he

dared. Here at last was the woman whose name he had heard mentioned many times before; the woman who helped George Fox send out circular letters; the woman who kept lists of the missionaries who were going out two by two over England, and even those who were going farther, to the Barbados Island or to America. It excited Tommy to think that the Stafford family was on her list. It must have been Margaret Fell, too, who had provided Fox with quill pens and paper to write his letters in prison.

There was a stir. The jailer brought in George Fox. The chief justice buried his face in the herb bouquet for a moment. "Jailer, take off this man's hat."

The jailer did so, and gave the hat to Fox. He put it on again.

"May it please the court, have I lain in jail for weeks and you object to nothing besides my hat? That is an honor God would lay in the dust, the honor which is of men, and which men seek one of another, and is the mark of unbelievers. Christ saith, 'I receive not honor from men.' All true Christians should be of His mind."

The chief justice replied in a stern voice, "I represent the Lord Protector Oliver Cromwell's prison. He has made me lord chief justice of England and sent me to this circuit to carry out the law."

"Do me justice, then," Fox said.

"We indict you as coming by force and arms and in a hostile manner into the court."

"This is false," Fox said. "The Friends carry no arms."

The chief justice questioned Fox a long time, but

Fox upheld God and his country in every question.

"If we release you, will you go home and stay there?"

"If I said so, that means I was guilty. My home would be my prison. I shall do as the Lord bids. I cannot submit to your request."

Tommy marveled. How could George Fox be willing to go back to the stinking prison cell? Yet Tommy knew why. God sustained Fox in every trial.

The circuit justice handed down his decision. "I order the clerk to prepare a passport of release," he said. "Take down my words: 'Permit the bearer hereof, George Fox, late a prisoner here, and now discharged, quietly to pass about his lawful business without any molestation.' I'll sign this with my own hand."

Cheers broke out from the usually quiet Friends. It seemed to Tommy that fresh air had swept in, although not even a door had been opened. George Fox had a key to his prison—the Lord's power prevailing over all. On his triumphant exit from the courtroom, Fox kept his usual dignity. Tommy wondered if his dismissal was the service to God Fox had meant. Would all the Friends in prison throughout England be freed because of the decision of the chief justice this day?

Tommy watched the jailer thrust a letter into Fox's hands.

"Read this at your leisure. I'm cleaning out every room in the prison house and putting new straw on the floors. My prison will be the best-kept place in all England."

The letter passed among the Friends later. "I can do no less than give thee an account of my present condition," the jailer had written. "God was pleased to make use of thee as an instrument to awaken me to a sense of life everlasting. I thank Him that He should have ordered thee to be my prisoner and to give me my first sight of truth. Pray for me that my faith fail not, and that I may hold out to the death, that I may receive a crown of life."

Tommy glimpsed the importance of Fox's mission in life as never before. Wasn't it possible that the service God wanted Fox to do was saving this one man? Prisons needed to be reformed in England. The jailer, with the new light he now had, would be starting a great service for his country in providing a clean place for prisoners to stay. Others in turn would imitate him. Tommy felt a sense of exultation and understanding.

Since George Fox had other plans for his ministry, he started on his journey after bidding the Friends from Ulverston and surrounding towns to carry the message of Christ wherever they went. The Staffords returned to Ulverston, and the inn became one of the places for Friends to meet.

One day at a meeting, Tommy saw Old John standing at the door.

"If it please thee," he told the Friends, "I have come to the meeting." He touched his hat but did not take it off.

The Friends greeted Old John warmly, as if they had known Old John a long time. "Welcome, Friend."

Old John smiled. "I have come for the truth." He beckoned to Tommy and whispered, "Master Dirk is outside in the coach."

Tommy ran outside, almost skipping in delight. He had so much to tell Dirk, he almost burst. "I'll take

the coach to the stable," he called, and drove around back. Inside, he unharnessed the horses and then flung open the coach door, laughing with exhilaration and excitement at seeing Dirk again.

Dirk stepped down, looked past Tommy, and gasped. There was a rustling sound from behind the feed bin. Two men stepped out of the gloomy shadows. "At your service, my lads." Black Bart himself stood before them, bowing low. Beside him, Stubby growled his annoyance at Black Bart's elaborate courtesy.

Tommy's only thought was to escape. He grabbed Dirk. "This way." He darted toward the door, but Stubby moved faster. He stuck out a foot and tripped Tommy. Both boys sprawled in the dirt.

Stubby prodded Tommy with the toe of his boot. "Get up," he hissed. "Don't try to run away. You're going to be useful to us."

Outside in the distance, men shouted.

"They're closer than I thought," Black Bart shrugged. "I hoped we'd lost them, circling around like this. Boys, it's hello and good-bye. We'd better take the coach horses," he said to Stubby.

The men's voices outside sounded louder and closer.

"We'll never make it," Stubby said. "They're surrounding us. And if they catch us with the money, we're goners." He paced the dirt floor. "Say, didn't a bunch of people go into the inn? What are they doing in there?"

"The Friends are having a meeting," Tommy said.

"That's our chance—our only chance." Stubby whirled to Black Bart. "We'll attend the meeting, too."

Stubby grabbed Tommy's shoulder with an iron grip and propelled him outside. Beyond the hedge shouts of the man hunters sounded only a few hundred feet away.

"Take us inside." Stubby motioned Black Bart to take care of Dirk. "Don't open your mouths."

Tommy led the way through the kitchen down the long hallway. The inn was absolutely silent, yet Friends sat everywhere—in the entrance hall, the broad stairway, and the long narrow parlor. They sat in Quaker silence. No one turned to look at the scuffling entrance of the highwaymen and the two boys.

A thundering knock on the front door was met with more silence. Constable Jarvis burst in, waving his men to stop behind him. He stared at the silent group.

"We've tracked some escaped prisoners thus far, folks. You having a meeting or something? Well, just answer me, Are you sheltering these criminals?"

"We obey the law," Father said.

Constable Jarvis nodded. "I can see you are those Quaker people. You don't talk or tattle on anybody and don't take off your hats to anyone. Well, men," he said, turning around, "I guess they're not here. You people can go ahead with your prayers."

From out of the corner of his eyes, Tommy saw Black Bart and Stubby pull their hats down over their faces, almost to their chins. Tommy longed to tell Constable Jarvis that Quakers took off their hats to God. Would the constable notice that two men in the room had not taken off their hats if everyone else did during prayer? But the constable, with a hurried look around the room and a disappointed expression on his weather-beaten face, turned away.

Tommy sat panic-stricken. Jumbled thoughts ran through his mind, but one point was clear. Black Bart and Stubby were two desperate men, who would be hanged if they were captured. They would not hesitate to use two boys as hostages in their escape flight. In fact, since the highwaymen had nothing to lose, they would not even stop at murder, if necessary.

Then, in the very depth of despair, Tommy remembered God.

"Show me what to do," he prayed.

10

In God's Service

The next moment Squire Grantham burst into the room, talking over his shoulder to the constable. "I don't care what they're having. My boy's gone. He may have come here to see that Stafford boy."

The squire saw Old John and stepped back in surprise. Old John curbed a movement to take off his hat. The squire stared at him, eyes narrowed.

"What, John? A Quaker?" The squire's voice quavered.

"Yes, sir, a Quaker," Old John said with pride.

Dirk made a wriggling movement and was almost on his feet before Black Bart pulled him down. But the motion made the squire look his way.

"Dirk, what do you mean coming here like this?"

As if inspired, Dirk said, "I'm a Quaker, too."

The squire sagged as if he had been struck. The silence of the entire group must have overpowered him. "Come home when you're through, Dirk." The squire no longer sounded overbearing. He backed out almost bowing.

Stubby shifted restlessly behind Tommy. "How long do we have to listen to this?" he whispered to Black Bart. "I don't understand a word he's saying."

"We'll take the boys as hostages and get out of here," Black Bart whispered back.

Tommy stiffened. The moment had come. If he and Dirk refused to go, they might be stabbed, but if they left, they would certainly find no mercy from Stubby. He would put his own safety ahead of theirs.

What would George Fox do in a threatening situation like this? Tommy knew without even asking. Fox relied on the Lord's power being over all. Yet Fox would not be passive, either, if there were something he could do that was in keeping with God's will.

Only one course lay open for Tommy. He could stand up as other Friends did from time to time when moved to bear witness. But when?

"The mighty day of the Lord is come and coming, that all hearts shall be made manifest; the secrets of everyone's heart shall be revealed with the light of Jesus," a Friend was saying.

It was all Tommy needed. He jumped to his feet. Dirk sprang up too.

Tommy hunched his shoulders and waited for the dreadful moment when he would feel Stubby's knife in his back. Instead, there was scuffling in the hallway, muttered exclamations of surprise from Black Bart and Stubby, and a triumphant hiss. "Got 'em! Take them outside. Don't disturb the meeting."

Tommy and Dirk hurried outside. Constable Jarvis and his men had already bound the two highwaymen.

"What made you come back?" Tommy asked Constable Jarvis.

"Something bothered me about their hats. I kept thinking the Quakers always keep their hats on. Then I remembered someone said they take off their hats when addressing God. I guess these two gentlemen didn't realize that." Constable Jarvis chuckled. "Then, too, their hats are the only flashy ones in the place, and their clothes, too, dripping all that lace and with those double cuffs. I still can't quite believe they'd dare hide in a Quaker meeting, but when you boys stood up, I saw something else." He pointed to his ear. "We didn't need any more clues."

Stubby cocked his head on one side, as if trying to hide his deformity. Black Bart, however, was as debonair as ever. "Well, boys," he said on his departure under the constable's custody, "come see us hang one of these days."

The boys watched until the highwaymen were out of sight.

"I'm tired," Dirk said. "Let's sit down."

They went to the stable and sat in the coach, reliving every incident of the exciting afternoon.

"When we go to Ireland, I'll really have something to tell William—that's William Penn, the boy I spoke of before."

"Oh, Dirk, I've something more to tell." Tommy had forgotten all about America in the excitement.

"To America?" Dirk's eyes flashed. "I hope I can go there someday—just to visit, of course. I know I'll have to oversee the estate here when I'm grown up. But George Fox said I would help seekers of truth. I wonder how it will come about."

Neither boy could think of what Fox meant, but Tommy had not the slightest doubt that the prophecy

112

would come true. Fox's prophecies always did. In the next two weeks, final arrangements were made for Quaker missionaries to tour England by twos. The Staffords were to go to London and meet Fox there. The morning before their departure, Agnes Buxby's son, a stocky, dark-haired young man, returned from the army and announced his intention of running the inn. "Anybody who wants London and its noise and dirt can have it. Ulverston is good enough for me," he told everyone.

When the Staffords were ready to leave, Mother clasped Agnes Buxby's hands in hers. "Everything is working out so well for all of us, thanks be to God."

"Aren't you afraid to go to America?"

"Why, no," Mother said. "We have a mission to do. We'll be so busy preaching the gospel we won't have time to be afraid."

"*We'll?*" Agnes Buxby asked. "You don't mean you'll preach, too, do you?"

"Yes," Mother said, "that is what I mean."

Agnes Buxby gasped and sat down. "I'm just a new Friend and I don't know all the ways yet, but I never in the world heard such a thing as this. It's outlandish—though I do have all the respect in the world for George Fox; yes, indeed I do. I'll never forget what he did for me. But women preaching? It's against the Bible, I'm sure."

"We don't think so." Mother was firm. "Besides, I'm not the first woman to preach. Elizabeth Hooton, one of the Friends, has preached for years."

"But won't you—" Agnes Buxby began and then stopped. "Oh, dear, I'm using the word *you* instead of *thee* and *thou*. I must remember the reason why I

113

must use the biblical form." Her thin face was wreathed in a gentle smile. Tommy marveled at the change in the landlady ever since God had healed her through the ministry of George Fox.

To the very last minute, Mrs. Buxby continued to comment on the Stafford's trip to America, in perfect goodwill as well as curiosity.

The Staffords left by horseback. Saddlebags of belongings hung on both sides of each horse. The late fall weather was crisp, Tommy had never seen so many grazing fields, meadows, pastures, woods, and heaths in his life. The roads had deep ruts. Sometimes they met a coach stuck fast in the mud, waiting for an additional team of horses from some farm cottage to come to the rescue.

It soon seemed to Tommy that he had been on horseback all his life. It was a relief to stop at a small inn along the way at night, but sometimes the Staffords were turned away because Tommy and Father did not take off their hats. Sometimes people in little villages stared at them. Some people spit to show their contempt. Others said, "With Quakers, their yea is yea, and their nay is nay. Good people they are, though odd in their ways."

Many days later, the Staffords came to London, a hundred times larger than Ulverston. There were long, crooked, dirty streets filled with coaches, liverymen, servants, young gentlemen ready to fight at the drop of a hat—or more likely still—at the insult of being pushed to the outside of the street where the contents of a slop bucket might descend on their heads from the apartments above.

Father found an inn where the family could stay.

George Fox had arrived ahead and was already preaching on the streets. The Staffords learned that many hundreds of Friends were in prison. There were hecklers and troublemakers everywhere the Quakers went. But now Tommy was a part of it all. He soon saw what it meant to be a Quaker.

The first time the Staffords went to a meeting place arranged for previously by George Fox, there was only one Friend standing at the door.

"What's the matter? Isn't there a meeting today?" Father asked.

The Friend looked up, tears in his eyes. "The constables came and arrested a great number of us and ordered the others to go home."

"Where is George Fox?"

The Friend brightened. "He's taking a statement to the printers—it's a letter against the harsh treatment meted out to us."

There was nothing for the Staffords to do but go back to the inn. When Fox came in later, he had already made plans for street preaching that afternoon. The Staffords went with him. A big crowd had gathered on a street corner.

Almost at once a heckler tried to make trouble. He addressed the people, standing in front of Fox and waving his fist. "I'm astonished that you people stand here like sheep and listen to a man talk about something he can't prove."

Fox's big bulk towered over the man. "Hast thou heard me speak before? What kind of man art thou," he said to the heckler, "to impudently say I can't prove my words? I say it is a lying, envious, malicious spirit that speaks in such a man. It is of the devil, not God. I charge thee in the dread and power of the Lord to be silent."

Tommy felt a strange exultation. He had so often heard Fox challenge unbelievers, and whenever he spoke in the name of the Lord, the mysterious power which Tommy had first sensed in Fox seemed to spread out and awe the hearers.

The man remained silent. The meeting went on. Afterward, Fox planned a meeting with Friends some miles out of London. They met there the next day, gathering in a large field.

A country constable, hand on sword, marched his men up to Fox. "In the protector's name, I command you to disperse."

"Why?" Fox asked.

"Tell me why you came here," the constable said in turn.

"I came here that the words of Christ might come to light, that by the Spirit all men might understand the Scriptures."

"You must leave here," the constable said.

"But what have I done?"

"We will not dispute with you. I've heard of your ways," the constable replied.

"Then hear what I have to say," Fox said.

"No." The constable jutted his lower jaw in a forbidding way.

"But Pharaoh heard Moses and Aaron, yet he was a heathen and no Christian. Herod heard John the Baptist."

The constable slapped his sword. "Withdraw!"

"I shall speak, for I have something to say."

"You shall not speak."

A scuffle commenced. One of the constable's men knocked Fox down, but let him get to his feet. During this time, none of the Friends made any noise. Their very silence seemed to infuriate the constable. He motioned to an assistant.

"Get the whip. I'll show these people what the law is. We'll whip all the Friends in sight. Are you a Friend?" he asked several. They nodded. Tommy nodded in his turn, and so did Celia.

The constable lined up the Friends. The Stafford family stood together near George Fox.

Tommy tried to hold himself still as he saw a long, snakelike whip whistle through the air. The constable's man was trying it out. The command was given. The whip cracked.

Tommy had a wild, sudden thought. "This is our first service to God." He braced himself for the blow.

11

Mistaken Mission

The whip descended with a terrifying whistle. Tommy tried not to wince, but the shock of the blow made his heart pound. To his astonishment he scarcely felt the next lash of the whip. In fact, he felt sustained by some wonderful, inner force, almost an exultation of spirit.

Four or five blows had rained on the Friends when a messenger arrived panting. "They're sending a troop of horses to break up the meeting," he said to the constable, pointing to the road behind him.

The constable withheld the next blow. Trumpets sounded in the distance. Two trumpeters rode up first, followed by a captain and soldiers on horseback.

"Divide to the right and left. Make way," the captain commanded the assembly of Friends. The captain rode through the gap to where Fox stood. "We'll take charge now," he said to the constable. "You may leave."

The constable's face sagged. He fingered his whip but turned away, reluctance in every step.

118

The captain stroked his pointed beard and looked over the silent group. "My orders are to break up this meeting."

Fox looked up at the captain. "Thou knowest by looking at us that we are peaceable," he said in his quiet way. "We have had many such meetings as this. If thou thinkest that we meet in a hostile way, search us. If ye find either sword or pistol, let the ones who hold them be punished."

The captain stiffened and frowned. "I'm here to obey orders. I will obey my superior's commands." His growing anger sounded out of place in the quietness. "If my orders were to crucify Christ, I would do it, or execute the Turks' commands against the Christians, if I were under them. I am here only to obey."

"Dost thou have orders against us?" Fox asked.

"I have orders to disperse a group of people plotting against the government."

Fox gestured toward the Friends. "Canst thou not see that we are an unarmed, peaceable people? Dost thou see a weapon upon us?"

The captain did not even look around. "No matter. I've heard tell of you Quakers. You are a cunning group. You should all be in prison."

"We have a thousand Friends in prison now," Fox said. "And for what? Because they live by the Bible, upon which the government of England is based? Because they are honest, their yea being yea and their nay, nay? Because they do not bow the knee to others? Because they do not take off their hats?"

Something in Fox's words and manner must have reached the captain's conscience. "What do you preach in the meetings?" he asked.

"I confess what Christ has done for my soul and what God's Spirit is ready to do for others."

The captain shifted in the saddle. "I'm sorry. My orders are to disperse this meeting, and I must do so. You must leave this place."

"Thy orders are—or should be—to disperse an unruly meeting," Fox said. "Look at these people. Dost thou see any violent movement among them? Any looks of hatred and uprising? Is it any honor to ride with swords and pistols amongst so many unarmed men and women?" Fox's rich voice was impelling.

The captain straightened as if he had made a decision. "Disperse or we will use force." He pointed to the road where he and his men had come. "Look there at what you've done."

A group of roughly dressed men approached slowly toward them.

"You have disturbed the lives of the country people, and they take such things ill," the captain said.

There was nothing to do but disperse. In groups of twos and threes the Friends started the long walk toward London.

By this time Tommy ached all over from the whip lashes. Each step hurt. He began to wonder about the exhilaration he had felt during the whipping and the pain he felt now. Why didn't Fox perform another miracle? Why didn't he draw on God's power and heal them all? Tommy could see that Father limped. Mother nursed a bruised face, and Celia cupped her hands tenderly as if trying to heal the wounds by touch. Fox himself had welts a half inch high on his cheeks. It would take weeks for the soreness to leave.

Tommy moved his shoulders gingerly, this time wincing at the pain. At the same time, he sensed an inner, soothing heat underneath. Had the healing process already begun? Then Tommy began to understand something about God's ways. Hadn't He set up natural laws of healing? Other people had to live by natural laws. Hadn't Fox chosen to suffer at times even when he could ask God to heal him by a miracle? Fox had said he must experience every condition in order to answer people's needs. How could he understand if he enjoyed special privileges from God?

As he thought about these things, Tommy felt a deep satisfaction. In a flash of understanding he grasped something more. Who but God had allowed him to understand? How would he know anything if God didn't permit it?

Mother and Father seemed to understand all this without speaking, but Celia, Tommy could see, was fighting back tears.

"Does it hurt very much, Celia?" he asked in a low voice.

"Of course it hurts very much," she snapped.

Tommy wanted to share his discovery with her. "Canst thou not feel a healing heat inside?"

Celia reflected. "Is God healing us already?"

"Yes, Celia. Let Him do the healing."

Celia held out her swollen hands. Then she tilted her head as if she were listening. Tommy could see she was experiencing what he had just discovered.

"Tommy," Celia burst out a little later, "I know now what it is to be a witness for God. I can't explain it." Her eyes filled with tears, but Tommy knew it was not from pain this time.

"I know, I know, Celia. God may let us suffer, but a person can suffer without being hurt. I mean—" He stopped, unable to explain. His words sounded silly. How could you suffer without hurting?

But Celia must have understood. She burst into laughter but it was tender. "I know, I know, Tommy," she teased with words he had just used the minute before.

She had hardly spoken when shouts sounded behind the Friends. The rough countrymen who had watched them at the meeting ran toward them brandishing sticks.

"There they are," their leader cried. "Where do you think you are going?"

"To our homes in London."

"You're not going fast enough. Come on, boys. Let's run them out of here." The group surrounded the Friends about twenty paces away.

Someone slung a small white object. It plopped on Tommy's chest with a crunch. A nauseating, sulphur-like odor choked Tommy. He knew what it was—a rotten egg. Tears stung his eyelids, not in pain, but in humiliation. He tried to wipe the egg off his clothes.

As if that were the signal, the country fellows attacked the Friends, throwing eggs, tearing at their coats, and pushing them to their knees. Someone slung a handful of mud from a ditch. Instantly, others did the same.

Torn, bedraggled, and muddy, the Friends kept on toward London.

"Witches—witches! Look at the witches," the rough men taunted. Apparently tired out, since the Friends offered no resistance, the men stopped and started back the other way.

Fox gathered the Friends together on the road. "All this ye do for Christ's sake," he said. "Ye are worthy of His presence."

Tommy felt the tingling sensation that marked the presence of God's Spirit within, together with a rapture and joy he had never known before.

A few nights later Tommy sat at supper with his family and George Fox. The talk had been on the coming mission of the Staffords and other Friends in America. Fox as usual ate very little. Now he sat back, a faraway look in his eyes.

"It will be soon now," he said, half to himself.

"Soon for what?"

"I have just felt taken. I had a sight of my being a prisoner."

Tommy stared in dismay. Was it to be the same story over and over? Would Fox always be thrust into prison, always having to defend himself, always suffering for the sake of the great power God had given him?

Tommy looked down at his plate. A feeling of shame rose in him. Hadn't he, too, known God's power when the whip descended? Hadn't God healed his wounds?

Fox smiled. "Yes," he said, as if reading Tommy's thoughts, "I have a suffering to undergo." He said the words in the same conversational tone he would have used in mentioning he had a crop to plant.

It did not surprise Tommy when Fox's prophecy came true. The very next night a Friend brought news. "George Fox, the justices and deputy lieutenants had a meeting and they issued a warrant for thy arrest."

"What care I about warrants against me?" Fox retorted. "If there were a cartload of them, they would not bother me. The Lord's power is over all."

Mother looked troubled. "Wouldn't it be better to leave London?" she asked Fox. "Then thou wouldst not have to be imprisoned here."

"Nay," Fox said, smiling. "They might fall upon other Friends."

The next day an officer with sword and pistols at his side strode into the inn. "I have a warrant for the arrest of George Fox. Which of you is he?"

Fox stepped forward. "I am the man."

The officer looked alarmed and clapped his hand on his sword.

"There is no need of arms," Fox said. "I knew of this last night. If I had wanted to, I could have gone forty miles before thou didst arrive, but I am an innocent man, and so it matters not what thou dost to me."

The officer looked from one to the other. "How did this news reach here? The order was made in a private house. You must have spies."

Fox smiled a little. "No matter how it was done, it is sufficient that I knew of it. Now, let me see thy warrant." Fox reached out his hand.

The officer stepped back, halfway drawing his sword. "You are to go with me to the officers and answer such questions as they should ask."

"But it is only civil that thou dost let me see thy warrant."

"No, I will not."

"Very well, then," Fox said. "It does not matter. I am ready."

Tommy watched the officer lead Fox away. This time Tommy felt something of the calm Mother and Father showed, and he knew the Lord's power was over all.

The news spread among the Friends in London that George Fox was unjustly committed to prison again, but it was not until the whole winter passed that Fox appeared in court. On the appointed day the courtroom was crowded with Friends and curious onlookers. The justices took their places. Fox stood before them.

The chief justice did not mention Fox's hat. "George Fox, you deny God and the church and the faith."

"Nay," Fox replied. "I profess God and the true church and the true faith."

"George Fox, you and your friends are embroiling the nation in blood and raising a new war. You are an enemy to England."

Fox raised his hand in protest. "I have nothing but love and goodwill for my country and desire the eternal good and welfare of England and its protector."

"There has been a plot against the country. Have you heard of it?" the chief justice asked.

"Yes, I have heard."

"Where did you hear?"

"Through the high sheriff of Yorkshire," Fox said. "I travel much over England. But as for knowing anyone in such a plot, I am like a child in that. I know none of such people."

"Then why did you write against plots and plotting

125

if you did not know some that were in such plots against the country?"

Fox threw back his broad shoulders. "Because the law tries to mash the innocent and guilty together; therefore, I wrote against it to clear the truth and to stop all forward, foolish spirits from running into such things. And I sent copies of it into Westmoreland, Cumberland, Bishoprick, and Yorkshire, and to thee here. It is likely to be in print by this time, for I sent a copy to the press."

The chief justice looked at his colleagues. "This man has great power."

"Yes," Fox said, "I have power to write against plotters."

"Then you are against the laws of the land," one of the other justices said.

Fox replied with his usual patience. "Nay, for I and my friends direct all the people to the Spirit of God. We are not against but stand for all good government, for good government does not stand in the way of freedom to worship God in the right spirit."

The justices conferred. At last the chief justice asked, "Are there any accusers against this man?"

Tommy held his breath. Would there be another ranter like Nick Hogan? To his relief, no one replied. George Fox was freed. His first action was to call a meeting of the Friends at the inn.

Once again the talk was of America. Someone mentioned the persecution Quakers faced there—lashings, imprisonment, and punishments. Someone reported that one Friend had an ear cut off.

At one time Tommy would have shuddered in fear at such a possibility, but now he knew he was ready to face whatever came. With an example like George Fox to follow, who could do less? Even so, he wondered why it was that the same punishment could be accorded a criminal like Stubby and to those who preached God's Word. He vowed to himself that he would learn about laws when he grew up and see if he could help make better ones.

But possible persecution was not the only problem the Quakers faced.

"Did you know that there is a hundred-pound fine on the owner of a ship that carries Quakers to America?" someone asked. "There is no ship willing to take even one Quaker across the ocean."

Nevertheless a shipowner did offer to take Quakers on his ship for a high fare. The Friends were delighted and confident that God had prepared the way.

Then came disappointing news. The shipowner could not fulfill his promise. A press-gang had forced his crew off the ship in order to serve in the British fleet. Turks had become a threat by attacking ships on the high sea, and England needed more seamen. The way to America was barred.

Tommy began to wonder. Had there been a mistake about Father's mission? Was Fox wrong? It looked as if God did not mean for the Staffords to go to America.

12

Unlocking the Door

The next day Tommy felt restless. He coaxed Celia to go with him to the Thames River and watch the sailing vessels arrive and depart. Masts and spars jutted skyward for miles. Sailors loaded ships, shouting to each other or to their companions, who climbed rigging or mended sails on the decks.

Tommy and Celia sat on the stone steps of a boat landing and watched.

"With all those ships, there ought to be one that would take Quakers to America," Tommy said with a sigh.

A soft, slithering sound behind him made Tommy turn. A brawny seafaring man with a round blue cap perched sideways on his head was descending the steps.

"America, did you say?" The seaman lounged against the stone wall. "What made you mention America?" His voice was casual, but his sharp eyes shifted from Tommy to Celia and back again. "I was just thinking of going there myself. You see that ship?" He pointed to a small sailing vessel anchored a hundred feet or so away. "It's mine."

"Can it sail very far?" Tommy asked. "It looks awfully small."

The seaman bristled. "What do you mean, small? That ship will ride the highest wave on the Atlantic. She's been across four times, and if I could get up enough passengers, I'd sail tomorrow." He cocked his head with a calculating air. His blue eyes and ruddy cheeks seemed to speak of stormy seas and high winds. "Perhaps your parents plan to go?"

Tommy found himself spilling out the whole story. Then he caught himself. Perhaps he should not tell these hopes to a stranger. "I mean, they have been talking about going," he ended lamely.

"What's stopping them?" The seaman's nostrils twitched. "Is it money?"

"Oh, no. It's not that," Tommy blurted. Celia nudged him. "I guess we'd better go, hadn't we, Celia?"

On the way to the inn, Celia scolded Tommy for telling so much to a stranger. "He looks like a schemer."

Later in the day, Tommy and Celia watched a procession with the lord mayor in his robes of black and red velvet at the head. Celia gasped. "Look, Tommy. There's that seaman we talked to this morning. He's watching the inn. I think he followed us here. Let's watch and see what he does."

In a little while Father left the inn. Tommy and Celia watched the seaman approach him and begin to talk. Tommy could see Father listening attentively. After a few minutes, Father returned to the inn, fol-

lowed by the seaman. A number of Friends were already in the main parlor discussing plans with George Fox. Tommy and Celia slipped in to listen.

"This is Captain Blayne," Father said.

At the word *captain*, all the Friends showed interest.

"Now, Captain Blayne," Father said, "please tell us about your ship."

Captain Blayne rubbed his weathered cheek. "Do I understand you people want to go to America?"

"Yes, we do."

"You're Quakers, are you?"

"Yes."

Captain Blayne pursed his lips. "It's against the law to carry Quakers."

"It is an unjust law. We can pay well," Father said.

"Besides that, the seas are dangerous the spring of the year," Captain Blayne continued. "Then, too, the Turks are a menace with their warships prowling the ocean."

"We'll take that risk."

Captain Blayne shot a quick glance around the room, then looked at the floor. "It's hard to get a crew these days, what with press-gangs stealing men off boats and putting them in the English navy."

"We'll all help with the ship any way we can."

"I'll have to consider." Captain Blayne shifted position. "How many are going?"

"About fifty."

"That'll cost you five hundred pounds."

The room was quiet.

"You see," Captain Blayne said hurriedly, "that takes care of possible fines."

131

"Very well," Father said. "We'll go. When does the ship sail?"

Captain Blayne licked his lips. "April 16."

The Friends agreed and Captain Blayne left with a satisfied smirk.

Afterward, George Fox decided to leave the next day on his preaching tour of England. The Friends gathered around to see him off.

Fox had a last word to Father about the mission in America. "Let your light shine among the Indians and the blacks and whites, that ye may answer the truth in them and bring them to their standard and ensign that God hath set up, Christ Jesus." He added, "It is a weighty thing to be in the ministry of the Lord God."

Father smiled. "It is not like customary preaching. Is it not to bring people to the Spirit which preaches within each of them?"

"Thou hast understood these things very well," Fox said. His farewell words to the Friends were typical. "Peace be unto all." He walked out of the inn without a backward glance, his bulky frame and white hat conveying a sense of strength and authority.

Celia began to sob. "We'll never see him again."

"But he's coming to America himself in a few years," Father said. "He told us so."

"By that time the Atlantic Ocean will be just like a highway—but no highwaymen," Tommy added with a grin.

"But I'm afraid they'll put him in prison again," Celia wailed.

Father was firm. "Has George Fox made any prophecy that didn't come true?"

Celia had to admit that he had not. She seemed satisfied.

Sailing day was a whirl of activity and noise. Sailors loaded Captain Blayne's ship with crates of live chickens, ducks, and turkeys. They rolled barrels up the gangplank, heaved bags and boxes into the hold, and stowed away foodstuffs—dried fish, flour, and spices. Tommy did not miss a detail. When the little ship finally set sail, he quivered with excitement.

The ship threaded its way down the Thames to the Downs toward the open sea. The first taste of real sailing did not last long. Captain Blayne ordered the ship to stop at Portsmouth, "to get more crew men," he explained.

Two or three seamen in loose trousers and full-sleeved shirts came aboard and looked over the ship. "No, too tiny. She'd never last on a high sea," they said.

Captain Blayne shrugged and set sail for the Atlantic, crossing without additional seamen. Scarcely a day from land, the ship sprang a leak. The crew and many of the Friends had to pump out water in the hold of the ship day and night.

Many of the passengers became seasick. For a while Tommy felt as if his stomach had parted company with his body.

Later, he felt better and joined other Friends on the wooden benches set up for meetings. The ship dipped and rolled in a soothing way, lifting with the waves.

One late afternoon the watch called out in a nervous voice, "Ship ahoy."

Passengers crowded the deck. "Where?"

"About four leagues astern," the watch said, pointing. "It looks like a man-of-war."

"Is it English?"

The watch hesitated. "No."

Murmurs and exclamations rose on all sides. "It's Turkish—a pirate ship."

"Is it following us?" Tommy asked Captain Blayne.

The captain scowled and did not answer directly. "Come, let us go to supper. When it grows dark, we shall lose it."

"But what if they catch up with us?" Tommy insisted.

"Don't worry about that," Captain Blayne said. But he looked concerned.

After supper, Tommy and Celia were first on deck. The mysterious ship loomed black against the sunset sky.

"Alter course," Captain Blayne ordered his steersman. The other ship altered course also.

"It's gaining on us," the watch called.

The Friends who had come on deck turned to Father. "What shall we do?"

"I am no mariner," Father said with a smile. "Captain Blayne, what can be done?"

Captain Blayne looked irritated. He paced a few steps. "There are two possibilities. We can either outrun it or tack about and hold the same course we were going before."

"But if it is a pirate ship," Father said, "We can be sure it'll tack about, too. As for outrunning it, there is no purpose in talking about that. Anyone can see it is sailing faster than this ship."

One of the Friends suggested, "But we can do

134

something. Doesn't the Bible tell us that if the mariners had taken Paul's counsel, they would not have come to the damage they did?"

Father agreed. "It is indeed a trial of faith. Let us therefore wait on the Lord for counsel."

The Friends sat down in silence. As in other Quaker meetings, the silence swelled and intensified. After a long time Father spoke. "There are those who want our lives, but they shall be carried away as in a mist. I see that the Lord's life and power is placed between us and the ship that pursues us. The best way is to tack about and steer our right course. Put out all candles except the ones the men steer by. Tell all the passengers to be quiet."

Captain Blayne gave the orders. "Cut through and steer your course straight."

At the eleventh hour in the night the watch called, "They are hard upon us."

Captain Blayne showed Father a map and traced a course across it in the wavering light of a lamp.

"Might we not steer this way?" the captain asked, a tremor of concern in his voice.

"Do as thou wilt," Father said. "We are safe now."

"Safe?" Captain Blayne gave a short bark of disbelief, yet when a contrary gale rose and threw the man-of-war off course, he had to admit that there was no more danger.

"The Lord has hidden us from them," Father told the captain.

"They have disappeared," Captain Blayne admitted.

On the First Day, Father called a meeting in the ship to give thanks for deliverance. "Mind the mercies of the Lord, who has delivered us, for we might have

135

all been in the Turks' hands by this time had not the Lord intervened."

Captain Blayne, standing near, disagreed in a loud voice. "That was not a Turkish pirate ship that chased us," he claimed. "It was a merchant ship going to the Canary Islands."

"Why, then," Father asked in a stern voice, "didst thou speak to me about this ship? Why didst thou trouble the passengers? Why didst thou tack about and alter course? Take heed that thou slightest not the mercies of God."

From then on, Captain Blayne ducked every time he saw Father approach.

"This is the way of unbelievers everywhere," Father pointed out to Tommy. "After God delivers them from great danger, they are apt to scoff and make little of deliverance. Take care not to do this. When God has wrought miracles, give Him the glory."

During the sixth week on sea, the ship reached harbor on the coast near Rhode Island. Everyone crowded the deck, exclaiming with joy at the green slopes and hills. Small boats skimmed out from shore to greet the ship.

The first boatload from shore stared up at the plain-clothed Friends.

"It's a shipload of Quakers," someone said, mouthing his disappointment.

"Sssh," an oarsman replied. "They pay promptly and never get into debt." He called up to the Friends on deck, "If you would like to land, we'll take you into shore for a reasonable sum."

"We thank thee, but we cannot," Father said.

His answer stunned the men in the little boats.

136

"Why not? Aren't you going to land here?"

"Yes, but it is the First Day. We cannot land until tomorrow."

The boatsmen rowed off muttering.

The next day, when Tommy put his feet on dry land, he was frightened. There must be earthquakes in America. The ground heaved and rocked. Celia and Mother staggered, too, and it was some minutes before Tommy realized that his own wobbly sea legs were at fault, not America. The other Friends had difficulty too, at first, but soon all were exclaiming at the neatly laid out village with its houses made of split logs and daubed together with mud.

Tommy looked around. "Is this—all?" He tried to keep the disappointment out of his voice.

Father smiled. "It certainly isn't another London."

The Staffords stayed with a Friend in the little town while Father arranged to have a log house built. The carpenter, a slight man with a wide mouth, was talkative. He had lived in Rhode Island for years. When he found out he was building for Quakers, he burst forth with opinions about religion at every opportunity.

"I've heard of you Quakers. There are some here. They're pretty safe in Rhode Island, but not in every place along this coast. Now, I hope you don't mean to tell me you've come over here with the idea of converting the Indians, as I heard tell."

"That is part of our mission, yes," Father said.

The carpenter threw back his head and laughed. "You haven't seen them yet—or smelled them, have you?"

"No," Father admitted.

"When you see what they look like and the awful smells they live around, you'll think twice about a mission." The carpenter measured off a length of timber, chuckling to himself.

Tommy thought of the prison smells in England, where there were no savages. After the horrible odors he had smelled in the basement room where George Fox had been imprisoned, he knew he could stand any kind of smell.

The carpenter was not through. "And don't try to convince me that Indians have souls."

"There is the light and Spirit of God in every person," Father said in a mild tone.

"All right. Let's put this to the test," the carpenter said. "There's an Indian comes in here to trade. He's learned English pretty well, but he keeps his Indian ways. Just ask him about that light in his soul. I'd like to hear what he says."

A few days later, the carpenter brought the Indian trader. He was tall, straight, and nimble, with swarthy skin rubbed with grease.

Father had Mother and Celia bring food. The Indian squatted and ate.

"Ask him about the light in his soul," the carpenter urged.

Father sat down on a log and motioned for Mother, Celia, and Tommy to sit near. He addressed the Indian. "When thou dost lie or do wrong to anyone, is there not something in thee that tells thee thou hast done wrong?"

The Indian looked thoughtful. "Yes, there is such a thing in me," he said, "and it makes me ashamed when I do wrong or speak wrong."

"And who or what is it inside thee that speaks to thee in that way?"

"I do not know. It is a strange thing." The Indian frowned with the effort of thinking. "Something is— what you white men say—locked up." He pounded his breast for emphasis. "White man has locks and keys and key unlocks door. I wish I knew how to let it out, whatever this thing is that tells me to be good."

As Tommy watched the Indian grunt over the effort of expressing himself, he felt himself struggling, too, trying to help. Then he remembered one of the first statements George Fox had ever made about earthly prisons and the other kind of prison, when the Spirit of God is not free.

"Father," Tommy burst out, "tell him about the key."

"The key?" Father asked.

"Yes. That's what George Fox called it. Christ is the key to the prison, he said."

"Who is this Christ?" the Indian asked in a humble voice, settling comfortably back on his heels.

As he sat listening to the Word of God, Tommy could see that God was blessing the Stafford family's mission in America. Their first conversion was under way.

THE END

The Author

Louise A. Vernon was born in Coquille, Oregon. As children, her grandparents crossed the Great Plains in covered wagons. After graduating from Willamette University, she studied music and creative writing, which she taught in the San Jose public schools.

In her series of religious-heritage juveniles, Vernon re-creates for children events and figures from church history in Reformation times. She has traveled in England and Germany, researching firsthand the settings for her fictionalized real-life stories. In each book she places a child on the scene with the historical character and involves the child in an exciting plot. The National Association of Christian Schools honored *Ink on His Fingers* as one of the two best children's books with a Christian message released in 1972.